THE
BLACK
PALM

BOOKS BY MICHAEL MCDOWELL AND JOHN PRESTON

THE BLACK BERETS

Deadly Reunion
Cold Vengeance
The Black Palm
Contract: White Lady
Louisiana Firestorm
The Death Machine Contract
The Red Man Contract
D.C. Death March
The Night of the Jaguar
Contract: Terror Summit
The Samurai Contract
The Akbar Contract
Blue Water Contract

THE
BLACK
PALM

MICHAEL MCDOWELL
& JOHN PRESTON

**BLACK
STONE**
PUBLISHING

Printed in the United States of America

ISBN 979-8-200-88188-8
Fiction / War & Military

Version 1

Blackstone Publishing
31 Mistletoe Rd.
Ashland, OR 97520

www.BlackstonePublishing.com

For Lt. Col. John David Friske, USMC Ret.

Boy! 't would have been my pride
To rear thy growing power,
And see thee towering by my side
In battle's glorious hour.
    —Lydia Sigourney,
     "The Indian's Burial of His Child"

1

Now, Rosie thought, *this is how it should be. This is more like it.*

Harry the Greek and Marty Applebaum were sitting across the table from Rosie. The big hairy Greek was listening to wimpy Applebaum go on about how wonderfully he'd blown up the guerrillas' sand castle in the desert. It had happened only a week ago, but Rosie'd heard Applebaum tell the story a hundred times already. But good old Harry just sat there and listened like it was coming fresh—like he hadn't been a part of it and nearly got killed himself.

Rosie took a big swig of his beer, leaned farther back in his chair, and let Applebaum roll. What the hell. They were back in America. Hell, they were in Shreveport, Louisiana—what could be more American than that?—in a honky-tonk bar where they didn't have to worry about somebody coming after them.

They were just three guys out for a few beers.

They didn't even have to think about trouble. They could just sit here and they could sip cold Dixie beer. Rosie didn't even care about the Confederate flag stapled to the wall above the jukebox.

Didn't care, because Rosie felt good. He looked around the room filled with plain ordinary American folks—mostly white, but a couple of red ones too, and this other black guy over in the corner—and he liked them all. Liked them 'cause he knew they weren't going to do anything to upset him. Wouldn't do anything that would make him climb back into his uniform. That uniform had seen enough business in the past few months. More than enough. That uniform had got torn and got dirty and got shot at in Laos and in North Africa, and both of them deserved a rest. You could practically hear that uniform snoring out in the closet out at Billy Leaps's farm.

Billy Leaps's farm was where they all lived now—the Black Berets. Where the team had come together again. There were five of them. Applebaum over there—he looked like a wimp, and he sounded like a jerk, but not one of those tales he told was made up. Rosie suspected that Applebaum might have exaggerated when he told stories about his conquests among the ladies, but the one thing old Marty had never had to exaggerate was a body count.

And Marty's friend—practically the only person in the world who actually seemed to like Applebaum—Harry the Greek. Haralambos Georgeos Pappathanassiou. But who's going to use a name like that at roll call? The Greek was big, the Greek was hairy, and the Greek carried around a lot of grief that you could see if you looked in his eyes—that's what you could say about Harry Pappathanassiou.

Rosie himself—just a big black guy who didn't quite fit in anymore. Not after Vietnam. Rosie'd done better than most after Vietnam—he got a job. And the job paid lots of money. Paid lots of money 'cause nobody else wanted to do it. Rosie worked in the morgue up in Newark. Not sticking tags on cold toes, that would have been easy. Rosie stripped the skin off corpses to use as bandages for burn victims. He got good at it. Didn't mind it. He had seen lots of death in Vietnam—he had been a medic, after all. And Rosie didn't mind working with corpses. They never gave you much trouble. Rosie tried to stay away from people who gave him trouble, 'cause Rosie had a temper. Rosie didn't like to lose his temper, 'cause somebody usually got hurt, and Rosie didn't like to hurt people. Just sometimes he couldn't stop himself.

And the two others who were still out at the farm tonight. One was Cowboy Hatcher, the pilot. Cowboy could have flown a dead mallard duck, once he'd picked the buckshot out. Three things made Cowboy happy. One was being up in the air, and nothing was better than that. But if Cowboy was on the ground, then Cowboy liked gadgets, the weirder the better. Cowboy had wired the farm like it was Fort Knox. A deer couldn't rub against pine bark without it showing up on one of those five green screens in the control room. The third thing Cowboy liked was cocaine. Any grade, any amount, any time. Went with anything, Cowboy said. When you said your prayers on coke, Cowboy said, God put down whatever he was doing and, God damn it, he *listened*. Problem was, Cowboy wasn't allowed coke—not when he was training, and sure as hell not when the kid was around the place.

And the last one. The team leader. The man who'd brought them back together. Billy Leaps Beeker. Not much to say about him. Half-Cherokee. Big guy, missing half his right ear. Got it blown off at Khe Sanh. Got it blown off by an overeager, too-scared American grunt—blown off while he was saving Rosie's life. Not much to say about Beeker, except Beeker was the reason they were all together again. Beeker was a *warrior*— no other word for it. And ten years after Vietnam, he had taken four miserable guys—who just didn't fit in anymore—and he had returned to them their warrior status. No, not much to say about Billy Leaps Beeker.

Billy Leaps had brought them together again, and now as the Black Berets they were a unit to be reckoned with. They had Washington agents crawling all over them, mercenary outfits begging them to sign on, military intelligence organizations realigning their plans to accommodate the possible onslaught of five men who together could wipe out an army. Who *had* wiped out an army. Twice—and that was just since Thanksgiving.

Rosie grinned, and Applebaum thought he was grinning at the story. Whenever Applebaum told a story he always added sound effects. Mostly explosions. But he could also do the cries of the wounded. Rosie thought Applebaum was just weird. So did the people at the next table.

An angry noise sounded through the honky-tonk bar, screeching high above Applebaum's explosions and the Dolly Parton wail on the jukebox. Loud jeering calls. A high-pitched scream. The hollow crash of metal. Rosie's entire body went on alert. Other heads turned in the bar. They'd heard it too.

Rosie stood up and punched Harry on the shoulder. The Greek looked up, and then followed Rosie's gaze toward the door.

"Hey, guys . . ." Applebaum protested. "Hey, Harry, listen, 'cause I'm coming to the good part, that was when . . ."

But Harry was on alert, just like Rosie. That sound was in his ears. Even if it hadn't been, Harry would have followed Rosie's path. One of his partners sensed danger and was walking toward it. Harry didn't even have to think. He went.

Marty followed, too, mumbling complaints under his breath. He'd get the asshole who interrupted his story. Rosie looked out the narrow doorway of the bar, his arms crossed over his chest. Harry stood behind him and to the right. Marty took up the third point of the triangle behind Rosie and to the left. He tried unsuccessfully to peer past the big black man's shoulder.

"Hey, what's happening out there, Rosie? Harry, can you see? All these guys think they got the right to interrupt my stories, just when I was getting going good, just when—"

"Shut up, Marty," said the Greek mildly.

But Rosie could see what was happening outside, and to the black man it looked like a real-life reenactment of a little piece of television history. A gang of teen-age whites swarming in the narrow, ill-lighted side street. They had blocked the path of a car paused at a stop sign. Two dozen white boys, some of them with baseball bats, links of heavy chain, tire irons, rocking the old Chevrolet back and forth. And inside the Chevrolet were a couple of teen-age black kids, a boy and a girl, their eyes wide with fear, both squeezed together in the middle of the front seat, as far away from the doors as possible. The two back windows had been shattered, but not knocked in. There were deep dents in the hood and the trunk.

It was something you might have expected in the '60s, but not now. Not fucking now. "Damn it, this is the eighties! And this shit should be over!" Rosie shouted.

Nobody heard him. The thunder of the baseball bats, the lengths of chain, and the tire irons beating against the car prevented that. The boys were only frightening the black kids inside the car now, and they were doing damage that it was unlikely a sixteen-year-old could pay for. But in a minute— Rosie knew how these things went—the white boys might decide to play a little harder.

Roosevelt Boone did *not* want to think about this stuff when he was only trying to have a quiet beer in downtown Shreveport. Harry the Greek didn't like to see Rosie get upset. Marty Applebaum was pissed off that his story had been interrupted at the best part. And none of the three Black Berets liked to see such uneven odds. As far as they were concerned, the only difference between these hoodlums and a cadre of Libyan terrorists was a few months of training and a reliable weapons supplier. The impulse was the same—to frighten, injure, or kill the innocent.

The three Black Berets moved silently from the door of the bar to the curb. Without words, without even a gesture between them, the men had identified the ringleader. The kid was wearing a Southern Mississippi letter jacket—obviously not his. He was too ignorant and probably too young even to have walked into that place. But he wasn't too young to swing a baseball bat and have it land hard on the Chevy's hood.

"Go back to your own place. Get the fuck out of our neighborhood!" he screamed savagely through the windshield.

This brought cheers from the rest of the gang, and they beat on the car as if it were one enormous metal kettle drum.

"This is *our* Shreveport! You got your own! Stay there!"

The cheers got louder.

God, bein' young can make you dumb, thought Rosie. Kid looked seventeen, maybe a year or two older. Good muscles. Not good enough, of course. Not to stand up to Roosevelt Boone. Rosie put a smile on his face.

The kid's baseball bat came back up in the air, ready to strike on the car hood once more. But Rosie had got there and his big, black hand reached up in the air and stopped the club from beginning its downward slam.

"What . . . ?" the kid murmured. He turned around and he saw Rosie. He did some quick thinking. Rosie could see it in his face. The kid glanced behind Rosie, and he counted two more guys, big white guy, little skinny guy. Just three. He looked at his gang. More than twenty.

The gang did the same kind of thinking, and then they

started to grin. Sure, that hairy white guy looked big and mean, but this nigger wasn't *that* big and that little blond man, hell, they could stomp him out in about two seconds. Rosie exchanged a single glance with Harry, and that glance said, *They think they've got a chance.*

Two battles started up, one on either side of the Chevrolet. Marty had moved into the group on Rosie's left. It was dark, but even if it had been broad day, it would have been hard to see just what Marty was doing. He moved that fast. A heavy exhalation of breath—*hooooofff*—meant Marty had just punched an adolescent gut like it had never been punched before. A muffled crack and a strangling in the throat was a broken nose. Marty threw punches the way he laid dynamite. With precision. And he was fast and accurate. Probably wanted to get back to his story, thought Rosie.

On the other side of the car was Harry. He just walked up to the kids, slow and sad. Like somebody inside the bar had just told him a real hard-luck story that he believed. The kids looked at those sad eyes and they probably thought, *Guy probably knows he's gonna get stomped.* One by one, in pairs, then in a group the adolescents assaulted Harry. They tried to get punches in. They tried to get behind him. They tried to throw a kick, or smash him with a length of chain. But Harry always anticipated, like the whole business had been choreographed, and he had been practicing it for weeks. He knew where every blow was coming from. Fists slammed not into Harry's gut but into the fender of the Chevrolet—and knuckles got smashed. Legs kicked empty air and were then grabbed and twisted—and some kid who had never felt real pain before tried to crawl away along the gutter. A length of chain whipped out at Harry's face and was just as quickly whipped out of its holder's hands and a half-second later it whipped back again and cracked a rib or two.

Harry didn't even seem to move fast, just slow and deliberate, taking whatever came, and giving it back again one better. His expression never changed, as if from afar, he were still listening to that same hard-luck story he really did believe.

Then there was a sudden hard sensation in Rosie's belly. That little fool with the baseball bat had tried to kick him. Rosie'd nearly forgotten him.

"I've had about enough out of you," said Rosie.

The kid with the Southern Mississippi jacket stared. He'd kicked the black man with all the force he could muster. The black man had hardly flinched.

"Haven't your mamma and daddy taught you that the races are s'posed to live together in harmony?" Rosie demanded.

The boy didn't answer.

"Well, I think they should," said Rosie. "Starting about five minutes from now. But until then, you and I are gonna have our own private race riot. You understand what I'm saying to you, boy?"

On either side of them, things had quieted down—except for the groans. The boys with their breath knocked out of them had pulled away, standing well aside behind parked cars or leaning in doorways. The few with bloody mouths or bruised knuckles or smashed noses whimpered on the curb. They probably didn't realize how lucky they were—the Black Berets didn't usually pull their punches. A number of the bar patrons now stood on the sidewalk, silently watching. So when Rosie spoke, everybody could hear him.

The kid made one last movement with the baseball bat. Rosie grabbed the kid's wrist and pushed it down so hard and fast toward the street that the bat smashed against the asphalt and split in two. The boy's arm and whole body vibrated painfully, and he bit the side of his tongue so hard that it instantly filled his mouth with blood.

"What's your name, boy?" Rosie demanded.

The kid spit out a mouthful of blood, and then replied in a snarl, "Bobby Lee Byrd."

"Well, Bobby Lee, what was you and your friends doing to this nice boy and this nice girl in this car here? Look at that poor girl—she's scared to death. And I don't blame her one little bit. Going out for a drive with her boyfriend, she probably didn't expect twenty hoodlums to jump out of nowhere and say they was gonna kill her. That what you expect every time you go for a drive with your girl?" Bobby Lee Byrd didn't answer. "Is it?" Rosie demanded.

"No," said Bobby Lee sullenly.

"No what?"

"No, sir," said Bobby Lee, and it was apparent from the expression on his face how much it cost him to say *sir* to a black man.

Rosie looked around. Bobby Lee's friends were watching to see what he'd do. Rosie knew Bobby Lee's type—the school bully, with a mean streak and a foul mouth.

Rosie knew the type all right. Hardly ever got the licking they deserved. That thought gave Rosie an idea. He grabbed Bobby Lee by the collar and dragged him around to the front of the car.

"Turn on your headlights," he called to the black boy inside the car. The black boy, still nervous, pulled on the headlamps. One of them had been smashed, but the one on the right still shone. Rosie hopped up onto the hood. The headlamp afforded just a little light in the dark street. Bobby Lee stood uncertainly, and was just about to twist away and run, when Rosie simply lifted him off the ground, and threw him across his lap. Rosie stuck his hand under the waist of the kid's pants and with one motion ripped them down.

There was Bobby Lee Byrd, who'd been a bully in Shreveport for more than ten years, with his bare ass across a black man's lap in a city street.

Rosie paddled his ass with the cupped palm of his left hand.

Paddled hard. Slow at first, to give the crowd time to realize what he was doing.

"Watch your friend, guys," said Marty, and he jerked one of the kids out from behind a car, and pushed him toward Bobby Lee.

Rosie began to paddle faster. The boy's buttocks had looked snow white at first. Now they were glowing red.

Bobby Lee Byrd began to moan. Then, as his friends gathered around, he tried first to tough it out, then silently pleaded for help with streaming eyes. The pain increased. Rosie could paddle hard. Rosie could go harder then softer, faster then slower, build it up and let it subside—and the pain just accumulated. Bobby Lee, aware now that no one would help him, broke. Pain, shame, fear of this man holding him helpless, broke him. Bobby Lee Byrd cried.

The gang had gathered round, and they stared at their former leader. One or two jeered at him, or just spit on the ground.

That's what Rosie wanted to see. He'd just deflated a bully for all time. But he kept on paddling. Bobby Lee Byrd deserved it. If the Black Berets hadn't been inside that bar, that black kid in the car would have ended up in the hospital. The girl would probably have been raped. When he thought of that, Rosie paddled harder.

Bobby Lee's body quivered in uncontrollable spasms. If Rosie had kept on, he could have made a real jelly of the muscles inside those buttocks. The rhythmic beating of his cupped hand could have broken down the tissue. But Rosie knew when to stop. So he did, suddenly, without warning. But the pain had built up inside Bobby Lee and Bobby Lee kept on whimpering. Rosie just lifted him and threw him several feet away onto a crowd of his former friends—the ones who were now actively jeering at him. They didn't quite catch him, but they served to break his fall to the pavement. Bobby Lee fell on his back, and his bruised ass scraped against the dirty street. He screamed in pain and tried to struggle away.

"Get that piece of shit out of the street," said Rosie, and immediately two or three boys dragged Bobby Lee over to the curb.

"All right, now," said Rosie, "we're gonna take up a little collection for this young man inside the Chevrolet. We're gonna make sure he has enough money to get all the dents out. So open up your pockets, guys."

Rosie hopped down from the hood of the car, snatched a cap off one of the gang member's head, and said, "Pass this around."

The gang members emptied their pockets, giving all the money they had. They weren't about to cross this man. When the cap was filled, Rosie reached into his pocket and stuck in half a dozen twenty-dollar bills. Harry gave what he had with him, and after Rosie gave him a look, so did Applebaum.

"All right, now everybody get the fuck out of here. And I hear about something like this happening again, I'm gonna know who did it, and not one of you is gonna get away with just a little nosebleed—you understand?"

The gang melted away as quickly as their injuries would allow them. Rosie spoke for a couple of minutes to the couple inside the car, and then the Chevrolet drove uncertainly on. The whole thing had taken something less than ten minutes.

"I want to finish my story," said Marty. "My beer's probably warm, too, and we just gave away all our money. That kid's gonna show up tomorrow night in a Continental."

"How much did you put in the hat?" Harry asked.

"Two thousand," said Applebaum sheepishly.

"Christ Jesus," laughed Rosie. "Marty, you are a jerk. Why the hell are you carrying two thousand dollars for a night out in Shreveport?" But Rosie knew the answer: Applebaum liked to show off. Always. About everything. And they had so much money, the Black Berets, that they weren't going to miss what Marty had given away.

They went back into the bar, and even though they didn't have any money left, the bartender served them without stint till closing time.

2

The two figures were running back toward the house in the slanting yellow sun of the Louisiana morning. They were clothed only in shorts and track shoes. Neither Billy Leaps Beeker nor Tsali showed fatigue, though they'd just pushed one another along a grueling six-mile course.

They moved with liquid grace. Their arms and legs were synchronized. Tsali was a full-blooded Cherokee with the long lean look of his race. His hair was longer than most sixteen-year-olds would wear it. He was letting it grow as a gesture of respect for his heritage.

Beeker's heritage was obvious too. Not just that half of him that was Cherokee and which had given him a deep-tanned appearance, strikingly black hair, and a nearly hairless chest—but also that other half of him that was the product of those other than the Cherokee.

He had his mother's blue eyes—in fact, that was all that he had ever got from her. Directly after his birth she had abandoned him to go on her extended tour of all the sleazy dives and red-light districts of the country. Her eyes were there in his head—cold blue and too wide apart. But there was also the military bearing. It was evident in the severe Marine Corps high-inside haircut that left only shaved bristle on the sides of the skull and then only slightly more hair on the top. It was a cut that seemed to emphasize Beeker's mangled ear, to say that he was proud of the disfiguring injury that had torn away his lobe.

Beeker and Tsali's chests heaved in protest against the hard run on the last leg of the journey. With Tsali's long hair flowing behind him, the pair made their way across the expanse of clovered fields that surrounded the house, then onto the soft and well-kept lawn, and finally they jumped up onto the big concrete platform at the top of the steps. They stood there for a few moments, leaning forward with their hands on their knees, working to force vast amounts of oxygen into the lungs—trying at once to convince themselves, one another, and their own bodies that the pushed run had only been a normal exercise. So that tomorrow they could push a little harder.

Beeker said nothing. There was rarely any need for speech with Tsali. Between them was great understanding. In any case, Tsali was mute. He'd never spoken a word in his brief life, and communicated only with signs.

Finally, they went into the house. At first glance, the place looked like the home of a well-to-do bachelor farmer. The construction was careful, but without excessive detail. The rooms were comfortably furnished, but anything that wasn't needed wasn't there.

The floors were fieldstone. They had walked into the very large—almost baronial—living area. The kitchen was exposed, cut off only by a waist-high counter. All the appliances there were expensive but purely functional industrial pieces of steel and chrome—no designer colors, no ice-water spigots embedded in the refrigerator door. The dining table occupied a large space just beyond the counter—it seated six exactly. The Black Berets and Tsali—no visitors came here.

Then the stuffed chairs and couches took up the other half of the room—upholstered in dyed leathers that would last far longer than any other material.

A practiced eye would have seen and judged—the minimum, but on what little there was, no expense had been spared.

The other parts of the house showed more peculiarities, however. Just beyond the living room was the large windowless space that housed all Cowboy's electronic equipment. His "toys," a skeptical Beeker called them. Screens and keyboards, flickering lights and the whir of mechanized consoles that provided a twenty-four-hour-a-day security system for the farm. A communication system that insured that none of them—not even Tsali—would be without the means to reach a man in the field or a source in Washington or any foreign capital.

But the most striking thing about the house was the line of smaller rooms that followed. Here was no sign of personal wealth, no hint of concern with personal comfort. The rooms that were used as sleeping quarters by the Black Berets and Tsali were no more than cubicles. Each one contained a hard and unadorned bed, a single closet, a single dresser, and—that was all. It was all that a warrior needed—and that covered all five of the Berets. It was more than a Cherokee boy who had never known a real home had ever even dreamed about—and that meant it was plenty for Tsali.

The older man and the teen-ager stepped quietly past the six bedrooms—four of the doors remained closed. It was still early in the morning and the others remained asleep. They went into the single common bathroom at the end of the corridor. As much as the cubicles, the bathroom resembled what you'd find in a barracks. Four stalls and opposite them were four identical sinks with a long horizontal mirror hung above them. At the end, a slight drop in the tile and there on the wall, four shower heads. All that a group of men really needed, but no more.

Beeker and Tsali stripped off their running gear and went to showers at the opposite ends of the line. The steaming streams of hot water quickly sent up a cloud of fog at that end of the room. They rubbed themselves carefully with soap, and Beeker said to Tsali, "Your hair too."

This meant that Beeker finished first. While Tsali was trying to get the soap out of his hair, Billy Leaps turned off the shower.

Beeker quickly toweled himself dry and now the pair moved back to their rooms. "Get on your underwear, then come in my room," said Beeker.

A few minutes later Tsali entered. Billy Leaps sat on the edge of the bed, scowling, pulling on a pair of black socks. He muttered, "Black socks. Goddamn lawyer thinks a pair of goddamn black socks is going to make a difference . . ."

Tsali grinned sheepishly, and looked down at the floor. Besides his Jockey shorts, and his bleached white T-shirt, he was wearing a pair of black socks as well.

Beeker stood up and from the top of the wardrobe took down several large cardboard boxes and put them out on the bed. He opened up the top box and took out two matching pairs of gray flannel trousers. He took the pair meant for himself and handed the other to Tsali. When they had stepped into them, Beeker pushed the box onto the floor, and opened the next. He took out two dress shirts, stripped off the wrapping, and began searching for pins. When this was done, they put on the shirts—Tsali winced when one last pin pricked his neck. Beeker pulled it out and said, "Always one more than you thought."

Beeker pulled back a couple of steps and looked at Tsali. The sharply creased new clothes looked good, he had to admit that. The kid's long hair . . . hell, he refused to tell Tsali he had to have a haircut. It was Tsali's quiet way of showing the pride he took in being Cherokee. The kid had lived in foster homes and juvenile centers all his life, the first and easiest butt of all the jokes, and the last one to receive any of the presents. A full-blooded Indian without the ability to speak, Tsali had been born with both hands wrapped around the shitty end of the stick.

And what happens to the boy now is up to some judge, who doesn't know . . .

Beeker took out the two ties he'd bought. Different colored stripes diagonally marking the pure silk would be the single difference in their outfits. *Should be me in my fatigues and Tsali in his loincloth*, Beeker thought. *Shouldn't be trying to fool people about who we are, we should be showing them.*

Imagining his lawyer's face if the two of them walked into the courthouse like that amused Beeker just enough to take the edge off. He handed Tsali his tie and then wrapped his own about his neck.

Tsali bit his lip as he studied the length of silk. He finally had to go over to Beeker and push his arm for attention. Tsali lifted the tie with a helpless expression.

"Suppose they don't teach you how to dress like this down at the juvenile farm," Beeker snorted. He turned Tsali around, and standing behind him, wrapped and knotted the tie around the boy's neck. "I'm not going to bother to teach you how to do this, because as soon as we get back today, we're gonna burn these fuckers."

Harriet Jopkins sat down in her leather chair behind the enormous, raised desk. Harriet loved that moment, that moment when she walked into the courtroom and everyone had to stand and acknowledge her.

It had taken years for Harriet to fight the whole system of judicial appointments in order to get this position. Years of being passed over by the old-boy network that controlled northwest Louisiana's courts. Years of being insulted by the petty remarks of stupid lawyers who never anticipated that a woman would be placed in a position of such authority. Years of being dismissed as a joke by the high and mighty men who ran the big law firms in downtown Shreveport.

Well, she got them back. Hard work, dirty fighting, persistence, and a liberal governor had won for her. And now she savored every minute of her work. She loved to see all the men who had put her down having to stand in front of her, call her "Your Honor," and bow to her decisions. Harriet had become known as the Iron Lady years before that British twit became prime minister of Great Britain.

Her eyes roamed over the courtroom. This was an easy day. Just a few civil cases, adoptions, the like. She saw Cynthia Martell, her friend and ally—her *only* friend and ally when it came to that—standing to one side of the county attorney's desk. Cynthia was always present at adoption cases.

With a nod of her head, a gesture withheld for a beat longer than necessary, Harriet gave the county clerk permission to intone his next command, "You may be seated."

The crowd noisily reclaimed their chairs.

Harriet shuffled through her papers as the clerk in his monotonous, obnoxious voice called out the first case to be heard. Harriet already had the papers in her hands.

Petition for Adoption
of Tsali Leaps Beeker
by William Leaps Beeker

Harriet looked over at the table where the two males in question sat silently. She snorted silently. "Mr. Lawry, your client is single?"

The attorney representing Beeker stood up. "Divorced, Your Honor."

Harriet scanned the papers and found the notation. *"Twice?"*

Lawry shuffled uncomfortably. Harriet Jopkins was the one judge he hadn't wanted to be assigned this case. Anyone with half a mind would have understood what a neat, uncomplicated way it would be for the state to be rid of the responsibility of caring for a sixteen-year-old mute Indian boy. It was a miracle that a boy of that race, of that age, with a handicap, would ever be adopted—it was surprising enough that he had never even been sent to reform school. But Lawry knew Harriet Jopkins and her dedication to the Family above all else.

"Boys need a mother," said Harriet. "Especially wild ones."

Beeker began to rise from his chair, in fury—automatic fury.

"The boy isn't wild," said Lawry mildly, motioning Beeker down again with a pleading glance. "Included in the report are his most recent school records, and evaluations of several teachers, Your Honor."

"All boys that age are wild," remarked Harriet, thumbing lazily through the report. "All boys need the moral influence of a mother. It seems to me—"

The lawyer couldn't keep Beeker down. He stood, his arms automatically assuming parade rest, clasped hard behind his back. His voice was slightly strained. "Ma'am . . ."

Harriet Jopkins looked up in vast surprise. The man was speaking wholly out of turn, and had called her "ma'am."

"Your Honor," whispered Lawry to Beeker. "Call her Your Honor."

"Your Honor," said Beeker. "It's the tradition of the Cherokee for the father to bear responsibility for the raising of boy children. Tsali is full-blooded, I'm half-blood. We want to live in the traditional way."

Harriet snorted again—this time aloud. *Indian ways?* The

Cherokee tradition was a bloodthirsty patriarchy. She'd let hell freeze over before—

But suddenly Harriet's eyes were sending strange messages through to her brain. She couldn't remember her usual adamant stance on adoption or what she'd meant to say next. Why? What was happening to her?

She had an actual physical response to the half-breed Indian standing before her. A liquid warmth in her lower belly. Why? Because of the way this man was standing? With his arms behind his back, his pelvis forced forward making Harriet look at his . . .

She flushed and stared back down at the papers. Then her eyes went back up again, without her willing them to. This strange man. Harriet shifted, rubbed her legs together beneath her black gown, hoping to ease some of the pressure she felt down there. But it didn't help, not at all.

The smart jacket and dress slacks couldn't hide the pronounced musculature of that body, not with the sinewy muscles in his neck, not with the way his thighs pressed against the material. But more than anything else . . . Why did he have to stand with his legs apart that way, his hips thrust forward as though inviting—no, *commanding*—Harriet's vision to the . . .

This was a man who should have the care of a son. Where did that thought come from? He was what all those boys in the juvenile hall needed. Not one of those wimps whose physical activity was limited to popping beer tops and lawnmowing once every two weeks in the summer.

"Do you two hunt?" she asked, turning suddenly to the boy. How had she known they did?

Tsali nodded, yes.

"You can't speak at all?" she asked, not unkindly.

"It's in the papers, Your Honor," Cynthia Martell spoke up. "He's been mute since birth."

"Tsali isn't the name that appears on your birth certificate," said the judge, after a moment. She wasn't the Iron Lady anymore, she was . . .

"Tsali," said Harriet, and there was a slight choke in her voice. She coughed to cover it. "Tsali, does Mr. Beeker take good care of you?"

Tsali nodded solemnly.

Harriet Jopkins bit her lip for a moment, but did not take her eyes from the boy. She didn't trust herself to look at Beeker anymore. "When you need him, is he there for you?"

Tsali nodded once more, and then made several hesitant motions with his hands.

The judge didn't know the hand language. "What did he say?"

Billy Leaps Beeker paused a moment, then, in a low voice, interpreted: *"He is already my father . . ."*

Harriet Jopkins paused a moment. When her words came, they were hurried and nervous: "Then you're a very lucky young man, Tsali. Adoption granted."

Cynthia Martell gasped audibly.

Harriet Jopkins turned quickly in her chair. "File your papers, Mr. Lawry. Court's adjourned for twenty minutes. Clerk, reschedule."

The Iron Lady fled the courtroom. Everyone stared after her in amazement—everyone but Billy Leaps and Tsali, who cared for nothing but the judge's assenting decree.

Mr. Lawry, who had sat between them, shook hands with Beeker and slipped away. Beeker and Tsali stood facing one another. Tsali's eyes glistened, but no tear formed.

He formed the sign for *Father*.

Beeker looked at him and swallowed hard. All he could get out was "Yeah."

3

Beeker brought the pickup to a stop in the parking area next to the house. He and Tsali sat there for a moment, staring straight ahead through the windshield. Legally and in the eyes of the world, they were now father and son.

Beeker had sensed the tie between them from the first moment he saw Tsali—being taunted and tortured by two Louisiana rednecks. The corpses of those two men were rotting beneath the forest loam less than a mile away.

The rope that bound them had grown stronger during the time that Beeker nursed a wounded Tsali in his home. It had tightened beyond his capacity ever to loosen it when he discovered that this adolescent Cherokee had shed his first mortal blood while defending Beeker's farm. Agents who had come to destroy the Black Berets' base of operations were instead wiped out by the kid's bow and arrow.

The fact of life and death—taking life and creating death—is the force that unites warriors like the Black Berets. When it crosses the lines of generations as it did with Tsali and Billy Leaps, the bond becomes that of father and son. No court was needed to verify it. The adoption decree wasn't so much for the state of Louisiana as it was a gesture by Beeker toward Tsali.

Beeker had known the fear of being abandoned as a youngster. His grandmother had been there for him, true, but her presence hadn't entirely made up for his father having died in Korea, his mother having taken off for a life of carnal self-indulgence. When Beeker was teaching physical education at the military academy outside of Shreveport, he had seen that skittishness and insecurity in too many boys. If this piece of paper would allow Tsali to calm down, and stop trying so hard to prove his worthiness to Beeker and the others, then it was worth a morning's outing, the struggle to wear the confining suits, and the lawyer's substantial fee.

Beeker and Tsali opened the doors of the truck cab in what seemed the same motion—they were that much in tune with one another. Under the noise, Beeker said aloud, "My son . . ."

Tsali whipped his head around—he had heard. He looked for one moment at his father, and then slid out to the ground.

It was quiet at the farm. Beeker and Tsali walked to the house, silently. Tsali stepped ahead of his father, and pushed open the door. He stopped dead in surprise.

Oh God, thought Beeker, registering the sudden tension in Tsali's frame, *somebody's come after us*. He started to grab Tsali out of the way, imagining rifle fire, imagining grenades, imagining death for his son coming in a hundred mangling, bloody ways. He would have thrown Tsali and himself off the concrete porch had he not immediately heard laughter from inside the house. Familiar laughter. And the pop of a champagne cork.

Beeker recovered himself, grinned a grimacing grin at Tsali, and pushed him into the house.

There were the other four Black Berets—Harry the Greek and Marty, big black Rosie, and Cowboy in dark glasses and

Stetson—holding up enormous glasses of champagne, and toasting Tsali.

Cowboy quickly poured two more goblets of champagne and brought them over to Beeker and Tsali. Tsali wouldn't accept his till he got a reluctant nod of permission from Beeker. Beeker took his own even more grudgingly.

"God damn it, Beak," complained Cowboy, "if you wouldn't let me go to the courthouse, standing in as a goddamn uncle or something, the least you could do is plan a little party. Buy the presents."

"*What* presents?" demanded Beeker.

"Hey!" cried Cowboy. "Here's to the kid! Tsali Leaps Beeker!"

The Black Berets noisily raised their glasses and drank off the champagne. Rosie was already opening another bottle.

"Cowboy," said Beeker, with an edge in his voice, "*what* fucking presents? Listen, Tsali's up to his ass in that electronic shit in there you're always buying. I let you set up that fucking TV over there and now . . ."

Cowboy pushed Beeker over into a corner of the room. Tsali looked like a diplomat shaking hands with Rosie, while Applebaum filled up his glass again with champagne. The boy's face was radiant.

"Listen, you half-breed bastard," said Cowboy in a low voice, "let the kid have a little fun, would you? He's probably never had a party thrown for him in his whole goddamn life, and you and I are not gonna spoil it with fighting. Now I got the grill set up outside, and Rosie and me are gonna cook us some venison burgers, and we're all gonna swill champagne till we're falling down drunk, and nobody's gonna say one thing that's gonna upset that kid over there."

Beeker was silent, which meant at least that he was listening to Cowboy, who had been his friend even before the Black

Berets got back together. Cowboy said things to Beeker that no one else dared.

"You may have signed those adoption papers this morning, Beak, but I tell you one thing—that kid belongs to all of us. So this is his day—okay?"

Beeker nodded once.

So they drank champagne, but long before they were through the case that Cowboy had bought, they had switched over to beer. They moved outside, into the back of the house, and Rosie and Cowboy cooked up the burgers made from the meat of a deer that Tsali had brought down with his bow and arrow. Marty got to tell his stories again—which now included the fracas outside the Shreveport bar. Harry fell asleep in the hammock that was strung between two pines. Rosie decided to drive back into Shreveport and check up on the black kids who had been terrorized the night before.

Cowboy and Beeker sat together, and talked quietly. Billy Leaps said without preamble, "All right, *what* present, Cowboy? More of your junk, I'd guess."

"Nope. A vacation."

"Where?" demanded Beeker, who didn't at all like the sound of it. "Doing what?"

"Just this little island in the Caribbean where I almost got married one time."

"The Caribbean?" Beeker sounded disgusted. "Tour groups and love boats and straw hats on fat old men—"

"And young ladies in itsy-bitsy bikinis." Then, before Beeker could register a protest, Cowboy added, "And lessons in scuba diving."

Beeker sat thoughtfully. Cowboy knew he'd won: the idea that Tsali might be denied any kind of physical training, any opportunity to expand his physical prowess, was torture to

Beeker. He had vowed not to spoil the kid, but he had also voiced his conviction that Tsali would never be denied anything that would help him turn his body and skills into those of a man.

"You and me and him," said Cowboy. "Already made the reservations. Already got his classes set up. I'm gonna fly us down."

"When?"

"Tonight." Cowboy grinned.

"The others?" said Beeker, nodding in the direction of Harry, sleeping, and Marty, babbling his stories to an enraptured Tsali.

"Rosie don't want to go. Rosie likes Florida—Pensacola, Santa Rosa, along there, where he did his training. He's going back there to do some fishing—and get away from all us white folk for a while, I guess."

"You worked this out, didn't you, you bastard, behind my back?"

Cowboy laughed his high-pitched laugh, and rocked back and forth in his chair. "You didn't suspect a thing! Marty and Harry are gonna stay here and guard the place."

"Marty's not gonna like that," said Beeker. "Marty's gonna want to be where the action is."

"There's a munitions show in New Orleans next weekend. He's going down for that. And lay the whole goddamn French Quarter—he says."

From a small speaker attached to the back of the house came a sudden beep-beep, repeated about five seconds later. Tsali ran for the back door.

Cowboy glanced at Beeker: "Somebody sending a message through Tsali's computer."

"Who? Somebody talking to Tsali?" He started to get up, but Cowboy shook his head. Beeker sat down again and waited impatiently. A few minutes later Tsali came out of the house with a single sheet with computer printout.

"Who the hell—"

Delilah, signaled Tsali, spelling out the name. He handed the sheet to his father.

Delilah's message was brief.

CONGRATULATIONS MR. TSALI LEAPS BEEKER. TELL YOUR
FATHER I NEED TO SEE HIM. D.

"This is the life." Cowboy sat on a lounge chair by the pool with a piña colada in his hand. He and Tsali had arrived on New Neuzen very late the previous night, after dropping off Beeker in Washington, D.C. As soon as Beeker had had his meeting with Delilah, he would join them on the small Caribbean island. He had no more idea than they as to what the lady might want. But Delilah knew things that no one else did, and there was nothing frivolous about her summonses.

"Isn't this the life?" Cowboy demanded of Tsali once more.

Tsali nodded. He wasn't about to argue. He and Cowboy were sitting side by side. Both wore swimming briefs. Tsali felt a certain strangeness about it all—but he loved it. For the first time, ever, he had a real drink in his own hand.

It was strange being off alone with Cowboy. Strange and exciting. If Beeker was his role model, his teacher, his idol, his *father*, then Cowboy was his big brother. The one who knew all about the forbidden pleasures and who posed all the temptations. Beeker took everything so seriously. Cowboy never seemed to take anything seriously. The two men were opposing forces in Tsali's life, but complementary. He loved them both.

Even with as little as he had drunk, Tsali felt a pleasant buzz from the piña colada. It was something he'd never experienced before. Not at all bad. He began to wonder why Beeker had always warned him away from this.

But what was most important about the drinks and about spending time with Cowboy was the rush of feeling like a *man*. Cowboy never spoke to him as though he were a child. He was always bringing up men things. Things like fighting and flying, drinking and . . . girls.

"Look at that one," Cowboy said in a low voice to Tsali. Even in his swimming suit Cowboy still wore his Stetson and his mirrored glasses. Tsali had a hard time following the other man's gaze. But soon enough he knew just whom Cowboy had to be looking at. "Now that's Grade A. That's something I could have served up on a plate three times a day and not get tired of it. I can smell the honey all the way over here."

She stood at the other end of the patio, on the far side of the pool, wearing such a tiny two-piece suit that it seemed a shame to bother wasting the foot of material that must have made it up. Three tiny triangles hardly covered the secret parts of her body—they were creased between her legs, and stretched over the points of her hard nipples.

Tsali felt himself get warm. His body pressed against the suit. He hated the way his sexual urges flowed through his body in ways he didn't yet understand. But his awkwardness seemed only to increase the tension, till he suddenly thought that his state of excitement was as obvious to those around the pool as the woman's anatomy was obvious to him. He quickly turned on his belly, nearly spilling his drink in the process.

"You ever had anything like that, Tsali?"

Cowboy's question was beyond Tsali's tolerance. He had never had *any* kind of contact with a woman. He had spent countless hours dreaming about them, wondering.

"What turns you on, Tsali? Come on, tell me . . ."

Tsali was mortified. It showed on his face and what Cowboy saw there made him sit up. The youngster still hid his head in the crook of his arm, hoping his embarrassment wouldn't show.

"Hell," said Cowboy in an awed whisper, "you haven't had it yet, have you, kid? Well, we're gonna take care of that. Right now. This fucking minute. Come on, get up, grab your stuff. We got some work to do!"

She was beautiful. Absolutely the most beautiful woman that Tsali had ever seen up close. Her skin was a rich chocolate, a well-mixed blend of her black, Dutch, and Carib ancestors. Her features were sharp, her nose small and pert. Her lips were thin and her eyes were remarkably blue—the blue of Dutch china. Her name was Ruth, and she was sprawled on the bed of a room on the third floor of this shining white mansion on the leeward side of the island of New Neuzen. The exterior of the house was whitewashed so that it gleamed in the surrounding lush vegetation. The unadorned interior walls were also gleaming white, and could blister your eyes where the sun shone through the windows and reflected off them. The floors were some unfamiliar dark wood, old, worn, and highly polished. A ceiling fan moved lazily above, and there was a trembling canopy of mosquito netting over the bed.

Cowboy had brought him to this place. Cowboy had conferred with the proprietress—an enormous, unhappy-look-ing fat woman in a brightly printed robe—and Cowboy had picked out the girl for him from among half a dozen who were presented for their inspection. And afterward Cowboy had taken two more of the girls for himself.

In the late afternoon the house was hot, quiet, peaceful.

"Come on, pretty man," Ruth cooed. "Take off some clothes. It is hot. Get comfortable. Come here." She reached out a hand, and parted the netting. She smiled, and the smile seemed genuine.

Tsali was trying to be adult about this. The woman had

seen men's things before. Why should he be so defensive about taking off his pants? But the hard flesh that was almost painfully trapped in his shorts wasn't buying it. It didn't want to be seen.

Ruth stood from the bed. She wore only a simple linen shift, tight and thin, that made it quite obvious she wasn't wearing anything beneath. She came out from behind the netting and slowly approached Tsali. "I know you cannot talk. I like that. I do not like to talk myself." She placed her perfumed head on his shoulder—a tender gesture. At the same time she lewdly pressed her hips against Tsali's, letting him feel the secret mound of flesh that he . . .

She drew back a step or two. Her fingers worked a couple of buttons on her shift, and it slipped to the floor. Naked, with her small, firm breasts pointing right at him, she walked back against his body, forcing his arms to surround and caress her. His shoulders tensed as he realized that she was undoing his fly and the button that held his pants closed. When she took her hands away, his slacks fell to the floor.

Ruth moved back a little to allow herself space to unbutton his shirt, to pull it off his shoulders and down his arms. Now there was only the white cotton of his shorts. He looked down and saw a wet stain there, the proof of his excitement.

She pulled him over to the bed. She fell gracefully back through the netting and onto the blue spread, and brought him down atop her.

The touch and the coolness of her skin! The warmth when his hips met hers!

At first there was a desperate desire to flee. To run away, back to the hotel and the sunshine by the pool. Then Tsali heard a noise—a sound from the next room. It was the slow rhythmic creaking of bed springs. Constricted breathing, soft moanings, and little encouragements in a Texas accent.

Just as Ruth was pulling at the elastic band of his shorts, Tsali understood that he was hearing Cowboy in the next room. He listened to the cadence of Cowboy's motions. As though he knew exactly what he was doing, Tsali began to follow them with the pulsings of his own hips. Ruth wiggled underneath him. "You are supposed to be new at this!" she gasped, her body pushing up to meet his thrusts.

Her hands were down there, directing him, guiding him. Tsali listened to Cowboy's moves, knowing they were the same ones he wanted to make. Just that way. He had been worried that it would all happen too soon, that he'd lose control. No more. He had an example to follow.

Just then Ruth's hands led him into a place of indescribable warmth and wetness. Deliciously he felt engulfed by her body, her flesh. He wanted to do it fast, to slam into this new treasure. But that wasn't how Cowboy was doing it. Tsali could hear. Cowboy was going slow. Gritting his teeth, Tsali followed the lead, working at the same slow tempo, using himself to lead Ruth on.

Her kisses showered on his neck, her arms dragged him down to her soft belly and breasts. Tsali felt a strange power, a new and unfamiliar control over himself. He lifted himself up and looked down to see himself driving the woman on. It was all in his body—not in his mind. He need not have worried. He suddenly stopped all his movements and was rewarded with a sharp sigh, a desperate plea. "No. No. More . . ."

But he stayed in position and made Ruth do the work, made her lift her hips in compliant need to fulfill her own satisfaction. Her breath quickened, her heat rose—and then Tsali pulled out and collapsed on his back.

Ruth was like a cat in heat. She jumped up and rolled over on top of him, her lips pleading with kisses. "What you want? Ruth give it to you. What you want, pretty boy?" Tsali smiled, hiding behind his inability to speak. He had figured something out. Let Ruth teach him, not because he was weak and didn't know the moves, but because he was strong and silent and if he said nothing, did nothing, then Ruth would have to find the ways to achieve her own satisfaction. He'd learned just what he might expect in the future. He was already sure that he'd want to do this again and again.

As he felt her mouth travel down his chest and over his stomach, Tsali listened to the quickening sounds in the next room and he imagined Cowboy getting just what he was getting, doing it just the way he was.

There was a sensation so strong in his body that he nearly lost his control. But, no . . . it wouldn't be right. He'd need time if he was going to learn all these things. He felt Ruth's mouth, her hands, her cool flesh as it moved against him.

He was going to have lots to speak to Cowboy about later. Lots.

Cowboy ordered another round of drinks in the hotel bar. He'd never seen Tsali look like this. Never. The kid had a big shit-eating grin on his face. And he was standing about a foot taller than before.

"So you like that, huh, kid?"

Tsali grinned wider and nodded, yes.

"Pretty good in the afternoon, is my opinion," said Cowboy. "Pretty good at night, and pretty good in the morning. I'm proud of you, kid. First time can be great—like it was for you. But sometimes it ain't so hot. But you really did it up, I could tell by the way that girl said good-bye. You know, most of the time, places like that, girls don't follow a fellow down three flights of stairs and out the front door." Cowboy grinned. "Hell, you could've moved in for the rest of the vacation and gotten it for free. Morning, noon, and night."

Tsali grinned at the high compliment. Tsali would have grinned at anything right then.

"I think we ought to send a wire to Beeker right this minute and say we popped your cherry."

Tsali dropped his drink on the slate tile and the glass smashed. *That* got rid of the grin. He was oblivious to the quick movements of the two waiters who came to wipe up the broken glass and spilled drink. His eyes were big ovals of terror, his mouth opened in silent protest, and for once he managed to stutter with his hands. Tell Beeker! No! He could never . . .

"Tsali, it's a joke. A joke . . . This'll be our little secret."

The youngster collapsed back on his chair in relief. If Billy Leaps found out what he'd done . . .

But Cowboy's mind had already moved on. He nudged Tsali, and pointed across the room. There, on the other side of the bar, was the beautiful woman they had seen at poolside earlier. She now wore a striped cotton robe over her bathing suit, but she had been joined by another woman—this one younger, even more beautiful, also in a bathing suit and robe.

"Hot, man, real hot . . ." Cowboy's voice had a faraway tone to it. "You passed your entrance exam, kid, with flying colors. You ready to move up to the next level?"

4

Beeker had never been to Delilah's house. But as soon as he saw it, he knew it was right. The place was in Virginia, about fifty miles southwest of the District. The hills in that part of the country were a gentle rolling landscape. They'd been cleared for centuries. Here the rich people rode horses just as they had one hundred, two hundred years ago. There was a sense of timelessness about it.

The earth had been worn down here. It had no sharp edges, no sudden peaks or valleys. Even the rivers and streams were placid and calming. Delilah didn't have one of the big Colonial period farmhouses so common in this area. Hers was—in comparison to most of the mansions nearby—a mere cottage. Just a low dormered farmhouse set on about a hundred acres of the most expensive farm real estate in America.

No show, nothing flashy. Lots of privacy, well-kept grounds. Even the power and telephone lines had been laid underground—nothing to detract from the essential elegance and serenity of the place.

Delilah—and Beeker expected this as well—lived alone. No

servant, no roommate, no lover, no husband, not even a body-guard. Delilah wouldn't want any of that. She wanted quiet, a retreat. Not to avoid the pace of modern life, but to energize herself so she could return to the fray confidently.

The door was open, and Beeker walked in.

The furniture was sturdy Colonial-style construction. There were plants, but only a few, not enough to overwhelm you. Flowers, but roughly beautiful ones, obviously from her own garden—Delilah wasn't the type of woman to spend money at a florist's for chemically produced blooms.

Beeker liked the place, because strangely enough it reminded him of his own home. Not that superficially Delilah's cottage and Beeker's farm were anything alike, but because they were both exactly suited to the owners—environmental extensions of those who lived there.

A fire blazed in the huge stone hearth that seemed to be way outsized for the small room. Delilah sat in a wing-back chair turned sideways to the flames. She was looking at him, waiting.

It was hard to remember that she was slim, that her waist was so small he could encircle it with his hands. She was wearing some kind of soft yellow robe and her large breasts caused the fabric to balloon out. He could make out the lines of her hips—full, fleshy, firm hips that had obvious strength to them. He was glad too that, because of the way she was sitting, he could see her well-turned calves.

He stood silently. He watched her, examined her. Thought about the times they had been together. That twitch in his crotch came back, the slow burning she invariably produced in his belly. No other woman could do that, even if she tried—Delilah only had to sit there.

His mouth was actually dry. His abdomen was increasingly enveloped in that growing warmth.

"We need you," she said simply. "We need your men."

Beeker studied her, but with an expression that wasn't a response to her words. It angered him that he wasn't in control right now, that he wasn't the one in charge. It wasn't simply a question of his being on her territory rather than his own. He never was in total control when he was with her. With Delilah he had to fight for position. It annoyed him. With anyone else, any other woman, he would have been able to clear his mind.

It was strange, he thought. Strange because she was the one woman in the world he utterly admired. The one person outside the team he came at all close to trusting. If Delilah said something was important, it was. But when Delilah was sitting there in a robe, a robe whose folds were open . . .

"Not yet," he said. "I'm not going to talk about this yet."

"What do you mean?" She was puzzled.

"I want you too much to talk. I'm too distracted to talk." Beeker delivered his lines with all the emotion and enthusiasm of a delivery boy who didn't expect a tip for the flowers he had brought to the door.

Delilah didn't argue. She stood up and came to him, pressing her body against his, wrapping her arms around his waist. She laughed somewhere deep in her throat as she laid her head against his chest. She lifted her head up to his, offering her lips, and with that motion, everything else he could want from her.

Beeker picked her up in his arms and carried her to the rug that was placed on the floor in front of the fireplace. He spread her body on the thick luxurious pile, arranging her limbs just so. He sat back a moment, gazed at her, and then spread open the robe. Quickly and familiarly, he touched all those remembered parts of her with a gentleness no one else could have expected from him. He kissed her again.

Beeker had put back on his slacks and his undershirt. With nothing else on his body, and his bare feet buried in the warm pile of the rug, he sat and drank the coffee that Delilah served. She was back in her chair, dressed in the same robe, holding the same pose he'd found her in earlier that afternoon. Their spent passion seemed to have left her exactly as she had been before. Unruffled, unmoved, the same woman with a job to do.

"What's the problem?" he asked. "Why do you need the Black Berets so bad? So sudden?" Beeker tried to seem as unchanged as she. He made his tone straightforward and matter-of-fact, perhaps even a little hostile.

He knew that Delilah wouldn't tell him the whole truth—even if she knew it. She was connected with one of the strange independent agencies that had spun out of the CIA and other federal intelligence outfits during the Carter administration when the function and efficiency of the secret services had been endangered. Groups had been formed hastily, all of them supposed to be able to carry on the surreptitious duties necessary for the survival of America. Some of them had worked, and done much good. Others had withered, or been disbanded when the CIA, the NSA, and the military intelligence groups had regained most of their power under Reagan. Still others had gone bad.

That whichever of these small, autonomous groups Delilah was connected with was on the side of the angels with big white hats straight from the agency was an article of faith with the Black Berets. Their only contact with the organization was through Delilah. They trusted her more than they trusted anyone outside the group, but that didn't mean that their faith in her was final or total.

Beeker didn't even know where Delilah stood in the organization. She might merely be an operative, assigned, for instance, to mercenary recruitment. Or she might actually be the head of the organization, with a hundred unseen men and women under her. There was also no knowing how big the outfit was. It might be made up of five, or twenty-five, or a thousand operatives and supporters—or it might be Delilah working with a computer and a Pentagon expense account. There was no way of knowing, or guessing. All Beeker knew was that when talking about her organization, Delilah said "we."

She took a sip of her coffee, and then began to speak in her official voice—as if she were delivering a lecture in a board room, with charts and graphs and a pointer, a secretary to take notes, and twelve men in business suits attending to her presentation. Instead, of course, she was just voluptuous Delilah, her skin color heightened from their exertions, wearing a yellow robe, curled in a wing-back chair with her feet tucked under her, staring into the fire.

"One of our ongoing concerns is of course international terrorism. We're particularly interested in investigating techniques of training, of cooperation between groups like the IRA and the PLO, of new devices, and of new strategies. Now, terrorists are a nuisance. They're even a danger. But everybody knows that Britain isn't going to topple a thousand years of democracy because of a bombing at Harrod's. And the PLO is going to have a rough time if its only goal is to push Israel into the sea. What we're afraid of—what we've been watching for, and planning against—is a terrorist group that finally gets smart and chooses a target commensurate with its size.

"That's what Parkes was going after in Bashi. You know that. He wanted his own country, his own seat in the UN, his own postage stamps, and a piece of real estate that could be leased out as a missile site to the highest bidder. And you stopped it."

Delilah paused, sipped her coffee, and smiled at Beeker over the rim of her cup.

"Something like that is going to happen again?" Beeker asked. "Parkes is dead."

"An entirely different group," said Delilah. "Someone we haven't heard from before. And that's why we're frightened, because we know so little about them. It's one thing to deal with the PLO and the IRA and the Red Guard, because they've been around—we know who they are. But these people—"

"You don't know who they are?"

"They're Indonesians. They were all part of a leftist movement in Indonesia, a leftover from the old independence group. When the country became independent, they were shunted aside. And for some obscure reason they blamed the Dutch, rather than their own people. They got kicked out of Indonesia, and went to the Netherlands—because as former colonial subjects they were automatically awarded Dutch citizenship. The Dutch are very permissive," Delilah added, but without apparent approval or disapproval in her voice.

"At any rate," she went on, "these Indonesian leftists all ended up together in Amsterdam, blaming the Dutch for their exile and their powerlessness. They wanted reparations, but all the Dutch would do is put them on the welfare rolls and take care of them much better than they were ever taken care of in Indonesia. So the Indonesians—a generally dissatisfied group—hijacked a few trains. They blew up a supermarket in the Hague. They poisoned a couple of reservoirs. And at long last the Dutch government got fed up and threw them in prison. But the Dutch made a mistake."

"What?" said Beeker, shaking his head. Permissive governments always did.

"They put all the Indonesians in the *same* prison. That gave them a chance to solidify their core group. They radicalized even further. And they didn't care at all about Indonesia anymore—they just wanted to get back at the Dutch government. They all made a pledge to one another, to destroy the Dutch government, and sealed it by tattooing the palms of their right hands. A black triangle—that's how you know them. They're now known as the Black Palm. They're totally vicious, I might add. They had a proper leader once but he got his throat slashed during a . . . a political discussion in the prison and the worst of them took over. Now they're just a bunch of proven killers with a grudge against the Netherlands."

"And now they're out of prison," suggested Beeker. He could easily guess parts of this story—he had heard similar tales many times before.

"And they're on the move," Delilah continued impassively. "They're going after the big time—they want their own country, and they've picked one out. The smallest and weakest of Holland's old colonies—a godforsaken little island in the Caribbean—"

Beeker's body tensed. Tsali was in the Caribbean now, with Cowboy, on some godforsaken little island. Pray to the god of the Cherokee that it wasn't the same one. "What's it called?" he demanded coldly.

Delilah hesitated only a second. "New Neuzen."

5

"New Neuzen!" shouted Beeker, standing up from the chair, spilling out coffee over the rug, flinging the cup away from him so that it smashed on the stone hearth.

Delilah stared at him. Her legs unfolded out from under her, but she didn't get up.

"Tsali's in New Neuzen," said Beeker, and started for the door.

"Where are you going?" she demanded.

"To get him out of there—"

"He's there alone?" She got up from the chair.

"He's with Cowboy."

She slipped between Beeker and the door.

"Then he's safe," she said. "Also, the Black Palm is gearing up for next week. That's our best information. There's no present danger. Not for several days. Nothing's going to happen in the next few days, and nothing's going to happen to Tsali while he's with Cowboy." Her voice was soothing.

Beeker still bridled, reaching behind her for the door. Then suddenly he stopped, and looked her straight in the eye. "You know everything. Why didn't you know Cowboy was planning on taking Tsali to New Neuzen?"

"I would have," she said, "if he had telephoned there. If he had made reservations of *any* sort. But I take it he flew his own plane there, right?"

Beeker nodded. "But he said he made reservations. He said he had signed up Tsali for scuba-diving lessons."

"Well he didn't," said Delilah confidently. "Because I don't have any record of it."

"I have to get down there," Beeker said. "Get me there."

"In good time," she said. "Go back and sit down."

He just stared. *Christ, the ink isn't dry on the fucking adoption papers, and I've already abandoned the kid to a gang of terrorists.*

"Tsali is fine," she repeated. "He's with Cowboy. The terrorists aren't going to do anything for several days. But we still need your help. Because we want them stopped for good."

Beeker kept shaking his head. All he could think about was Tsali on the island, ignorant of the danger there.

"We'll get Tsali out," she promised.

Beeker blinked. Despite his fear, despite his misgivings, he believed her. He believed she wouldn't lie to him.

He went slowly back to the chair, and tried to sit but couldn't. Instead he took up a place at the hearth, standing at parade rest, with his back to the fire. He watched her closely. If she was lying, he'd catch it in her eyes.

Delilah continued. Her voice now was no longer matter-of-fact, it had a tinge of grimness to it.

"Our government can't do anything, because nothing's happened yet. Not one incident. It would look like an incredibly hostile action if we were to send in troops at this point. After Grenada, we looked fine. After New Neuzen, we'd look like capitalist Huns."

"What about New Neuzen itself?" Beeker asked, trying desperately to turn his mind to something besides his son. "Don't they have an army?"

"They have a police force trained to round up pickpockets and prostitutes. There hasn't been a murder on New Neuzen in fifteen years, and that one happened on a tour boat. No standing army. No weapons to speak of. A concerted terrorist attack could take over the whole island in three or four hours, and that includes a break for rum punch."

"What's the government like?"

"They have good government. A democracy—a real democracy. The whole country votes. The prime minister is a woman, took over about eight years ago when her husband died, and has already been reelected twice. She's better than he was. Nobody's got a word to say against her, except that she's antimilitary, anti-U.S., and anti-Soviet. Wants New Neuzen to be left alone. Next year she'll probably be up for a Nobel peace prize."

"She's anti-U.S. and she's antimilitary, but now she needs the Black Berets," said Beeker with harsh sarcasm.

"She doesn't know anything about all this yet," said Delilah. "Oh yes, and about payment for the Black Berets . . ."

Beeker looked up in surprise. He started to wave this away. Where Tsali was concerned, to think about money was a sacrilege.

Delilah divined his thought. "I know. But we'll get Tsali out of there, and you'll still have your work to do. And you deserve payment for that work. New Neuzen is a poor country—practically everything they have is plowed back into agriculture or the promotion of tourism. So they don't have anything to spare. Mrs. VanderVolt's budget for the whole nation is probably what Shreveport pays for garbage collection. But don't worry, this will be worth your while. The Black Palm pulled a series of bank robberies in Belgium and northern France a few years back, and so far as we know, they still have the money. Negotiable currencies. So if you find it, it's yours."

Beeker listened to all this with impatience. He just wanted to get started. From a drawer in a cabinet on the far side of the room, Delilah brought him a stack of folders held together with blue tape. "What you'll need to know about New Neuzen. Practically all there is to know."

"I'm gonna call Tsali and Cowboy and tell them to get out of there."

"No telephone calls," she said flatly.

She went into her bedroom, and closed the door behind her. Beeker slit the tape, and looked at the different maps of New Neuzen, wondering only where his son was now, trying to pinpoint his location and gauge his safety. He was still looking at the maps when Delilah came out again, dressed in a rather severe green suit.

"Let's get started," Beeker demanded.

"Of course," she replied smoothly.

"For New Neuzen . . ." he said, waiting for confirmation.

"Not exactly," she said. "I'm taking you to your hotel so that you can change clothes. I want you to look nice. This afternoon we're going to have tea with Mrs. VanderVolt."

6

Cowboy opened his eyes. *Fucking sun!* It was only eight o'clock in the morning. What the hell was he doing waking up this early on a vacation? Especially with this hangover! He rolled over in the bed and closed his eyes, hoping the distraction of the sunlight wouldn't keep him from falling back to sleep. But then he heard the sounds that must have disturbed him in the first place. It was the noise of a man exercising.

Cowboy sat straight up. "Tsali, what the hell are you doing?" His voice was scratchy, his throat desert-dry. There, at the foot of the bed, was the kid. His body bobbed rhythmically into view, then just as rhythmically disappeared.

Cowboy crawled painfully to the foot of the mattress, dragging the sheets behind him. From there he could see that Tsali was doing push-ups.

Cowboy collapsed back onto the bed and pulled the covers over his face. But now that he had moved, he couldn't ignore the dull ache of his head, the foul taste in his mouth. He needed water. He needed water or a drink or . . .

He staggered to his feet and moved unsteadily to the

bathroom. He opened the tap and splashed the running water all over his face. He shook his head in a vain attempt to clear it. He toweled his face dry and cursed Beeker again. Cursed Beeker for making him give up cocaine. No hangovers on cocaine. Sometimes you woke up with a bloody nose, but that was nothing compared to a hangover made out of rum.

He cupped his hands and caught handful after handful of water and drank the cool liquid down. He felt more alert, but that didn't mean better. That meant more conscious of his pain.

He went into the bedroom again, and just as he entered Tsali jumped up with a smile. The exertion barely showed on his face. He started to do twists.

"Wait a minute! Wait a minute!" Cowboy held up a hand. "You got to talk to me about all this."

Tsali froze his motion and looked at Cowboy. He moved his hands more slowly than usual—Cowboy could follow his sign language only haltingly, and Tsali often had to break down and write his friend a note. *I have to do my work.*

"Your work! This is a celebration, a vacation. And you know what celebration means? It means you don't have to—"

Tsali shook his head vehemently. *I promised I would do my work. And today I must go for lessons in the water.*

"You really going after that shit?" At that point, Cowboy couldn't imagine that anybody in the world would want to do anything other than find a nice quiet grave in the shade. "Why don't you wait till we get back to Louisiana? You can sneak off with Harry and Applebaum. They were in the SEALs, they know all that stuff . . ."

I promised my father, Tsali signed, as a final reply.

Cowboy didn't press the point. When Tsali and Beeker started on their father-and-son rap, there was no stopping them. He shrugged. "Go on then, finish up this foolishness. I'm going to take a shower. We'll get some breakfast and then find you a teacher."

Cowboy certainly did wish that Tsali weren't so perky. He wished the little town of New Delft where their hotel was located weren't so bright and noisy. The sunlight hurt Cowboy's pale blue eyes, even with the cover of his dark glasses. The musical but loud voices of the natives assaulted his ears and ricocheted inside his brain. The warm air encouraged the stinking sweat on his body. Hell, *scuba diving*.

They marched onto the one long pier in the secluded harbor of New Delft and Cowboy read the various signs advertising boats for hire, island guides, and diving lessons. Cowboy had lied to Beeker when he said he had the lessons all lined up for Tsali—the whole goddamn idea had been spur-of-the-moment. So he had to find a teacher for Tsali before Billy Leaps arrived in New Neuzen. Money wasn't an issue. Money was something the Black Berets had plenty of. But Cowboy wasn't going to give it to some fool who was there just to rip off tourists. He knew that if Tsali was going to do this, he'd want to do it right. Cowboy also knew that Beeker would kill him if he entrusted Tsali to an incompetent.

But Cowboy also wanted to find someone fast. That was important. Because as soon as he got Tsali set up, he could go back to the hotel, find a lounge chair and a waiter who'd bring him endless glasses of rum-and-tonic to take care of this hangover.

When they came to the little rickety stand, Cowboy instinctively knew it was the right one. Doc Wilhelm's School of Diving. The sign was printed in seven languages. Cowboy wasn't even sure what all of them were. One had to be Dutch, one certainly was English, German, French . . . And what the hell was that? Malay? Who cared? What was important was the way the old man stood.

He was ramrod stiff beside his plain advertisement. His skin was jet black. His clothes weren't the best but they were immaculately clean and freshly pressed. Cowboy knew he was a soldier. He just knew.

Cowboy walked right up to Doc Wilhelm and stuck out a hand. "Giving lessons today?"

The old man smiled, crinkling the aged skin on his face and showing a row of gleaming white teeth. "Sure. Got me the best gear. Got me a good boat. Don't got me any students this morning." The smile turned into a grin. "Ain't very pretty, am I? Ladies from the hotel—they want someone pretty to show them how is done. They want to play games with pretty boys, and I ain't a pretty boy—am I, sir?"

"Mister, you're flat ugly," said Cowboy complacently, "but all the kid wants to do is learn scuba diving and learn it right. If you can teach him ugly don't matter."

"I one time teach sailors in Queen Juliana's navy. I can teach this boy."

Amazing, Cowboy thought as he realized just how naturally he had chosen Doc. He thought that Beeker's military sickness must be catching if Cowboy himself, hangover and all, could walk the length of the fucking pier, crowded with boats and booths, and tourists, and hawkers, and teachers, and guides— and pick out the one man who used to be a diving instructor in the Dutch armed forces. Amazing.

"Tsali's his name." Cowboy made the introduction and watched the two of them shake hands, hands across generations. "Thing is, boy can't talk. He's smart as can be, and he'll learn real fast, but he can't talk."

"You write and read?" the black man asked Tsali. The boy nodded. "That's all then. Can't talk under there anyway." Doc Wilhelm pointed at the blue waters of the ocean as if he held sole say in the matter of their use and deployment. "I'll teach you the signs, and there's a pad you can use. I read English pretty real good."

"All right," said Cowboy, "about the money . . ."

"I send you bill up to hotel," said Doc dismissively, without even glancing at Cowboy. He was already herding the goddamn kid onto his tiny boat.

Cowboy was amused. He knew what was going on in the old man's head. Here was this old vet, this man who'd taught the elite of the Dutch navy. Now he was pensioned off, stuck on a little backwater island that was "independent" and had no use for his real skills. Forced to spend his days with those tourists he hated. Didn't sleep nights for remembering what had been. Suddenly, there's this kid different from all the rest. A kid who was obviously going to become a warrior, and Doc Wilhelm had one more chance, an opportunity he had never thought would come around again.

No wonder he didn't care about the money. Doc Wilhelm probably would have taught Tsali for free. Paid for the privilege.

There, on the sun-bleached pier, Cowboy stood and watched as Doc Wilhelm explained to the boy about the equipment. Pointing it out, naming it, putting it in Tsali's hand, showing him how it fit, how it hooked up, how it should work—and Cowboy felt a little wave of melancholy come over him. *That's what I could be like some day. Old and hanging around some backwater airport giving sightseeing thrills to a bunch of polyestered suburbanites. Then, if I was lucky, there'd be this kid come along who'd want to learn how to really fly! And that's how I'd treat him—like Doc Wilhelm is treating Tsali.*

But all that was too heavy for Cowboy at a time like this. And his head *hurt*.

"So look . . ." he began, but neither Doc Wilhelm nor Tsali heard him. He shrugged, and wandered slowly back to the hotel.

7

"Aw, come on, Tsali. It's a fucking vacation. Especially since Beeker's not here yet."

I have to go to bed early. I have a lesson tomorrow.

"I know you have lessons. You have a lesson in the morning after you do exercises. And you have a lesson in the afternoon, before you run your fucking six miles. I should have known better than to turn you over to that relic of a Dutch DI."

He is a good man. A good teacher.

Cowboy knew he'd gone too far. Tsali, damn him, was as loyal as they came. This old guy Doc Wilhelm had caught him nearly as good as Beeker had. All his war stories. All his tales about the ocean. When the kid wasn't under the water, he was listening. Cowboy knew he had as much hope of breaking down that loyalty as he had of convincing Tsali that Beeker was a Russian spy.

"Okay," Cowboy conceded, "this is a vacation for me. It's a goddamn endless training session for you. That's fine. You're sixteen, and you can take it. But there's this other thing you could use a little more practice on. You get my drift?"

Tsali got it, and grinned.

"Can't neglect it," Cowboy went on, "or you'll forget what goes where. I'll have to find somebody to teach you all over again. And let me remind you, Tsali, you don't use that thing, it starts to shrink . . ."

Tsali looked horrified, and Cowboy hastened to assure the boy that he was only kidding. "But you do got to stay in practice. Now listen, while you've been down there getting your skin wrinkled with that old black goat, I've been doing a little investigating. You know those two ladies we saw the other evening—you know which ones I mean."

Targets, signed Tsali, a little sheepishly.

"Yeah, that's right," laughed Cowboy, "targets. We're gonna shoot our arrows right in their direction. Okay, so here's what I found out . . ."

Cowboy had maneuvered Tsali out of the room, and they were walking down the hotel corridor, in the direction of the bar.

"Stepmother and stepdaughter, that's what those two are. And the husband and father is a real pain in the butt. So stepmother and stepdaughter are supposed to be chaperoning each other. Which means they'll *both* play, as long as we can get 'em separated. And that's where you come in."

Tsali looked up in Cowboy's face, trustingly. For a very brief moment, Cowboy was embarrassed. But he got over it. "Do it for me, Tsali. Do it for your old buddy. Get the young one away for a while. Keep her occupied. Find something you both like to do, and do it. Do it twice. You got me?"

Tsali was grinning. It wasn't just the memory of the things that had transpired with Ruth at the gleaming white house around the corner of the New Neuzen coast—though those thoughts were certainly very appealing. It was also the way that Cowboy was treating him. Like a man, a member of the team.

All right, he thought, *but I have to go to bed early.*

"That's my man!" Cowboy laughed. They had reached the bar. "Waiter, two rum-and-tonics! And no cherries."

Seating themselves beneath an umbrella just outside the glass doors of the bar, they were able to watch the sun setting over the Caribbean. As they waited for the two ladies in question to appear, Cowboy filled Tsali in on the further results of his investigation: "See, this lady—name's Amanda—wanted a little money, a little security. Old Dandridge gave 'em to her, and all he wanted in return was a hot piece of goods on his arm. Public display, not private consumption, so the lady gets it where she can. The whole family's been down here before, and Amanda's always on the lookout for a little free-lance help. And I am just the man. That is, if you take care of the stepdaughter . . ."

Cowboy loved nothing more than a woman who was categorically unattainable. It was a relief to him to know that Amanda Dandridge wouldn't want to get married. When a woman did want to get married—especially if she were Latin American—then Cowboy all too often gave in. He loved weddings and he loved honeymoons. But the accumulation of wives in the course of the years was a problem. There were places in South and Central America where Cowboy, to put it politely, wasn't welcome anymore. Or if he was welcomed, it was at the barrel of a shotgun.

But a woman who was already married to a man who had something to give her—something like a reckless amount of money—she pleased Cowboy particularly. He could have his romance, his dash of danger added to it, and he didn't have to worry about putting another marriage certificate on the pile he kept in his closet at Beeker's farm.

The stepdaughter—her name was Jocelyn—was supposed to guard against her mother's indulgences. Old Dandridge had made it clear that he expected his wife to cater to the brat's needs, in partial return for her extravagant upkeep. But Tsali, well, Tsali could take care of Jocelyn.

Cowboy looked across the table at the kid. God, he'd fleshed out since he'd come to live with the Berets. The food, the good living, the constant exercise, all of it had added pounds to a frame that had been painfully thin when Beeker had first found him. Sixteen, and looked older. He still had some of the awkwardness of adolescence about him, but he knew how to cover it when he had to.

Tsali could handle the brat.

"Mr. Hatcher," said Amanda Dandridge, offering her hand limply. "How nice to see you."

Tsali was stunned for a moment. Oh yeah! Cowboy was Mr. Hatcher—his real name was so seldom used that it sounded foreign to Tsali's ear.

The two males stood up and greeted the two women. Jocelyn was cool, blond, cold. Tsali remembered her type from school—untouchable. But Jocelyn was far beyond the coldest, blondest, aloofest girls that Shreveport had to offer. She was rich. She knew it and she made other people know it. When Jocelyn saw what she wanted, she walked right up and took it down off the shelf. That included dresses, jewelry, and men. A few months before—hell, a few days before—Tsali would have been terrified to stand even as close to her as this. But he had Ruth under his belt, and that gave him confidence.

Jocelyn eyed him as if she were looking at a price tag, or a label that would tell her he was one hundred percent something-or-other.

Tsali glanced at Cowboy. He and Amanda Dandridge were pretending the meeting was coincidental. From her expression when she glanced at her stepmother, Jocelyn didn't believe it for a minute. Tsali reached into his hip pocket and brought out a small pad of paper and a pen.

When at Cowboy's suggestion they all four sat down, Tsali placed the pad and the pen between himself and Jocelyn.

"What's that for?" she asked.

Tsali wrote, *I'm mute. This is how I have to talk to you.*

She turned the pad around and read the message.

"Can you read lips?" she asked, forming the words carefully.

I'm not deaf, he wrote. *I just can't talk.*

Tsali had had many different reactions to his disability. Some people were frightened of it, others were intrigued. A few were disgustingly sympathetic. Once in a while he got one like Jocelyn—someone who was almost pleased by his handicap. Jocelyn was one of those people—she needed someone to take care of and Tsali would do just fine.

Just as he expected, she reached across the table and put a hand on his wrist. "You must have a terrible time of it." Underneath some female facades lurks a mother desperate to emerge. Nothing could bring out that maternal drive like a male with a disability—especially one that didn't get in the way once you got the man in bed.

And Jocelyn was that type. Somehow Tsali knew that instinctively. Or, if it wasn't instinct, maybe he had just begun to pick up attitude and moves from his pal Cowboy. In any event, Tsali didn't protest the way he would have if a man had hinted that he wasn't capable of a full life. Instead, he bowed his head, and hoped he could keep from smirking.

Jocelyn's hand went to Tsali's neck. She rubbed it tenderly. "Amanda," she said, turning to her stepmother, "he's mute. He can't talk."

"That is too bad," said Amanda briskly, then leaned forward and resumed her conversation with Cowboy.

"You poor guy," said Jocelyn, and seemed to mean it. "You want to dance? Can you dance?"

He allowed Jocelyn to lead him out to the dance floor. The band was playing a slow song, and Tsali put his arms around her. A little while later, when they returned to their table, Cowboy and Amanda were nowhere to be seen. But if Jocelyn even noticed, she didn't comment.

"You know," she said, "we ought to find something to do tonight that doesn't involve talking. I don't want you to have to use up that whole pad of paper on me . . ."

8

If Mrs. VanderVolt had known about the happenings on New Neuzen, she might have been more inclined to appreciate the figure of the man who sat in the drawing room of her country's small but elegant embassy. But Mrs. VanderVolt knew only what the CIA and the NSA and the Dutch secret service—such as it was—chose to tell her about international espionage. That wasn't much, and Mrs. VanderVolt knew no more about the Black Palm than did anyone else who read five newspapers a day, and remembered the outrages in Holland from several years back.

Beeker wasn't entirely sure what was happening on New Neuzen either, but he did know that this woman was a pain in the ass. She was that type of black lady who maintains an air of moral authority about her, like an expensive perfume that only complemented the natural odors of her body. He could put up with that, that and the way she sat ramrod stiff in her chair, drinking her tea and listening to Delilah talk. He could appreciate everything that Delilah had told him about this woman on the drive up from the country—that she was one of the most respected women in the world, that she headed one of the least corrupt regimes in the Third World and the Western Hemisphere, that she was intensely proud of herself, her heritage, and her country. But Mrs. VanderVolt was still a pain in the ass because she wouldn't be moved by Delilah's persuasion.

"I am so sorry," said Mrs. VanderVolt, who had learned a precise and rather Teutonic English in Amsterdam, "but I cannot see that there is sufficient cause for me to extend my visit here. I would of course, though at some other time perhaps, very much enjoy viewing Mr. Beeker's farm, and my minister of agriculture and exports would no doubt benefit greatly from an exposure to the latest techniques in the cultivation of rice and sugarcane. I, too, am very much interested in the subject, but I must confess that my technical expertise in the field is severely limited."

Mrs. VanderVolt counted among her faults a tendency to speak in full, rounded paragraphs.

Delilah glanced at Beeker, and Beeker just smiled a redneck smile. He wasn't going to help her out of this one—he was still angry at the delay in getting to Tsali. And now Delilah wanted him to go out of his way, and deposit this head of state on the farm . . .

"Madam Prime Minister, really, I must assure you that it *is* the opportune time, and we—"

The woman waved away Delilah's protestations once more. "I really cannot go. I have been too long away from New Neuzen." She smiled enchantingly. "And I really do miss it . . ."

What we should do, Beeker was thinking, *is gag her with that big silk scarf, tie her hands, and carry her out on our shoulders.* There were only a couple of guards—hell, Delilah could take care of those stand-up comics who were the prime minister's "protection." They were so skinny . . .

Beeker looked over at them. On the ride in to the city Beeker had read some of the material Delilah had given him on New

Neuzen. He knew that it—like many other Caribbean islands—was a melting pot of races, many more than Americans usually knew about. These guys were obviously from the East Indies. The pair had a look about them that even Beeker might have pegged for American Indians if he had met them on the street in Shreveport: the tan skin, the dark eyes . . .

He let the women talk it out. Delilah was of course attempting to deceive the prime minister. Delilah wanted Mrs. VanderVolt out of the way when the Black Berets went into action in New Neuzen. A simple deception. But simple deception wasn't Beeker's style, and he wanted no part of it beyond pretending to be a big-acre Louisiana farmer, sitting there uncomfortably enough in the embassy drawing room. Didn't have to fake *that* part. Didn't have any—

Then he was on his feet. So fast he hadn't thought about it. Only later would he be able to explain it to Delilah. How he had been thinking these guys were East Indian, that they weren't much for soldiers, even for a puny state like New Neuzen—then the sudden registration that they both had their hands on their pistols. They were pistols that Beeker had thought were only for show, something to flash and keep the lady safe. But then the guards were looking at one another very carefully, and Beeker knew that look.

It was the look of two men checking their timing and their willingness to go through with a job. They were readying themselves for a coordinated move. They had got as far as secretly unfastening the snaps that held the covers of their holsters. They had their hands on the butts of the pistols. They were both lifting the guns from the cradles of leather, and they were both going to shoot.

Beeker was already halfway across the room. As though his mind were computerized he took in all the factors without conscious deliberation, and then automatically assimilated them.

Distance, speed, accuracy, options . . . He dived toward the one on the right, both hands extended. He grabbed hold of the man's hand just as it was bringing the pistol up. He stopped the arcing motion before it was completed, before it could possibly aim the pistol at the expected target—the prime minister, Mrs. VanderVolt.

It was the two men who screamed—not Delilah and Mrs. VanderVolt. Beeker had the one man down. His own element of surprise was complete, and the shock of his preemptory attack had thrown both assailants off. The one he had attacked first never got a chance to respond. Beeker had the pistol flying through the air in one moment, he had slammed the guy's head against the marble floor the next, and then—for good measure— had slammed his knee into the guy's balls with such force that he blacked out so as not to have to deal with the intense pain.

The second guy made a mistake, which was to pause long enough to select his target. For a split second he had to choose between Mrs. VanderVolt and Beeker. He decided on Beeker, turned his arm, and fired.

But Beeker wasn't there anymore. Beeker was down low, aiming his head for the second guard's belly. When Beeker smashed into him, the guard was propelled back five or six feet against the damasked wall. The first bullet had embedded itself in the back of an antique couch. This second bullet shuddered through the plaster ceiling with a hollow *thummp*.

The air was knocked out of the guard's lungs as he hit the wall. He hit the floor, limp, helpless. But Beeker wasn't going to take the chance that this was a guy who could easily recover. Beeker stood up quickly, assuming a position that would have allowed him to repel any physical attack. When none came, Beeker reached out and grabbed the man's hair, lifting the speechless frightened face from the floor, and then—as though the skull were a football he meant to send spiraling over the goalpost, Beeker let go of the hair. With all the strength of his powerful leg behind it, the steel toe of his heavy boot caught the sagging head right on the chin.

There was a sickening sound of splintering bone. Blood spewed from the man's mouth and ears. His body lifted up from the floor, arms flailing, and when it fell back down, the head rolled in that particular way that defined just what a broken neck was. The corpse twitched a few moments, and then was still.

Beeker turned to face the women. Delilah had no expression on her face. What had happened was what she always knew would happen if danger presented itself while Beeker was around. The danger was eliminated. She probably wasn't even thinking of the dead man on the floor—the man whose face just wasn't there anymore after his jaw had been shoved up a couple of inches into his brain.

The prime minister, however, was wide-eyed. With shock, perhaps with fear. She still held her cup of tea upraised, but the handle had slipped around her two fingers, and the staining liquid had spilled out onto her skirt.

"Mrs. VanderVolt," said Delilah, "now I really *must* insist that you make that agricultural inspection of Mr. Beeker's farm."

The prime minister wouldn't look at Beeker. Then he realized that she wouldn't do so because he was standing so near the two bodies on the floor. Beeker moved away from them, and—following his expectations—Mrs. VanderVolt glanced in his direction, and with a curt nod said, "Thank you, Mr. Beeker. I imagine that you just saved my life."

Just then, two black men in business suits flung themselves into the room, panting, frightened. They were about to speak, but then they saw the two bodies on the floor. They looked up wide-eyed at the prime minister. She'd recovered herself.

Not bad, thought Beeker.

"I'm all right," said the prime minister. "I'll speak to you later about who these men were."

"No police," said Delilah in a low voice to Mrs. VanderVolt.

"No police," repeated Mrs. VanderVolt. Her two aides backed out of the room, perplexed and sweating.

When they were gone, Mrs. VanderVolt looked down at her lap where she'd spilled her tea, and grimaced at the mess. She put her cup aside, and delicately wiped at the stain with a napkin. "I was almost a victim," she said evenly, almost casually, "and I would have been but for Mr. Beeker's timely interference. But I won't be a dupe. Obviously neither of you is what was originally represented to me. So please explain to me who you are—who you *really* are—and why you so very much want me to visit Mr. Beeker's farm in Louisiana." She poured herself another cup of tea. "Of course I realize Beeker may not be your real name, that you may not own any farm at all, and that you intend on taking me to someplace that is nowhere near Louisiana."

Beeker smiled—maybe it just took another woman to get the best of Delilah.

Delilah looked back at Beeker. He spoke. "My name *is* Beeker, ma'am. Billy Leaps Beeker. I do own a farm. And it's in Louisiana."

"Do you raise rice and sugarcane?"

He shook his head no.

"I'm to be taken there for my own protection? Is that it?"

"Yes," said Delilah.

"So . . ." said Mrs. VanderVolt. "I take it there are more than two persons who are out to kill me. If there were only two," she said, waving her hand in the direction of the corpse and the unconscious man beside it, "I wouldn't have to worry anymore." She put her napkin to her nose—the stench of blood was rising in the heated room.

"There are many more," said Delilah. "Mr. Beeker, would you show Mrs. VanderVolt the hands of those . . . gentlemen."

Beeker went over and turned over the hands of the two bodies. On the right-hand palm of each was tattooed a black triangle, with equal inch-length sides.

"This has a meaning, I take it," said Mrs. VanderVolt. "Is it occult?"

"Terrorist," said Delilah. "They're called the Black Palm. Indonesian, and rabidly anti-Dutch."

Mrs. VanderVolt smiled grimly. "It would take a great deal of energy to be anti-Dutch for any length of time. I tried it once, but they wore me down. They are, after all, a good people . . ." The prime minister's smile faded suddenly. "I have no intention of fleeing from terrorists. If these Black Palm fanatics are on my island—"

"They intend to kill you," said Delilah. "They intend to destroy your communications. They'll poison your water supply. And they'll murder every tourist they can find. Their aim is to take complete control of New Neuzen."

"All the more reason I should be there," said the prime minister tartly. It was evident to Beeker that the black lady was maintaining her calm at a cost. Mrs. VanderVolt felt for the people of that island the way that Beeker felt for Tsali. He could see that. And suddenly he felt like helping her very much.

"My son is there," said Beeker suddenly. "And my best friend."

The prime minister looked up, puzzled.

"A coincidence," said Delilah quickly.

"Then Mr. Beeker, perhaps you and I should take the first plane back to New Neuzen. I would be honored to visit your farm on another occasion. And see the fields on which you raise neither rice nor sugarcane."

Delilah glanced angrily at both of them. "Madam Prime Minister," she said quickly, "all we want is four days. Nothing is scheduled to happen before the end of that time. We'd like to clear these people out before *anyone* is killed, before *any* damage is done to your island's infrastructure."

Both the prime minister and Beeker laughed at Delilah's use of the jargon.

"Our infrastructure is very fragile," said the prime minister, with a sly glance at Beeker. "I'm not sure that it could support the landing of five thousand Marines any more than it could support the depredations of the Black Palm."

Delilah sat back and smiled. "We're only sending in one Marine, Mrs. VanderVolt."

"One? We're small, I know, but—"

"Mr. Beeker will go, Mr. Beeker and a few of his friends."

The prime minister glanced at Beeker, who once more had moved away from the bodies on the floor. The man who had been knocked unconscious was stirring a little now, softly moaning. There was blood staining the crotch of his pants—Beeker had evidently crushed one of his testicles, if not both.

"Mr. Beeker and 'a few of his friends' hardly sounds like the customary U.S. method of intervention. No disrespect, Mr. Beeker."

"Mr. Beeker has been successful before," said Delilah hastily. "We only want you to give him the chance. In four days we will take you to New Neuzen, no matter what may have happened in the meantime. But for right now, we'd like to keep you safe and out of harm's way. Just four days, Madam Prime Minister. Please."

"I have no reason to trust you, or to believe anything you say." Mrs. VanderVolt sat still for a few moments, and sipped her tea. She looked at Beeker, then at Delilah, then at Beeker again. "If I refused, I have the feeling I'd be bound and gagged and taken to Louisiana anyway. And though I know that the authorities of the U.S. are not commonly in the habit of laying hands on visiting heads of state, the plane ride might prove uncomfortable. May I ask Mr. Beeker a question?"

Delilah nodded her head.

"Mr. Beeker, is all this the truth? On the level, I believe the phrase is."

"It is as far as I know. I can vouch for myself."

"Are you also able to vouch for this lady here?" asked Mrs. VanderVolt, indicating Delilah.

"She hasn't betrayed me yet," said Beeker.

"I've gotten warmer recommendations," grumbled Delilah.

"I prefer honesty to warmth," said Mrs. VanderVolt. "I will visit Mr. Beeker's farm, for four days. I take it that you have already prepared the press releases explaining my extended absence from New Neuzen." Delilah nodded. "I thought you might have. Was I right about the ropes and the gags? Would you have used them?"

Delilah was silent.

"Four days," said the prime minister. "It is difficult for me to believe how much trust I'm putting into one man. Mr. Beeker, I only hope that you will eventually be able to visit New Neuzen under pleasanter circumstances. It is an ideal island for romance."

"This time," said Beeker with a smile, "I think I'll be traveling without female companionship."

Delilah shook her head decisively, but smiling almost for the first time in the course of the entire interview with the prime minister. "I couldn't very well pass up four days in a tropical paradise . . ."

9

Doc Wilhelm scowled as he headed the small boat out into the blue pristine waters of the harbor of New Delft. "You didn't seem the kind of boy who'd oversleep on me. I thought you wanted these lessons!"

I do. Tsali and his instructor had worked out a very primitive sign language.

Doc Wilhelm snorted in a way that defied translation, but needed none.

The boat puttered; the warm sun and splendid views quickly erased the old man's displeasure with the boy. He knew that you only got this upset with a kid you had begun to expect too much from. It was only the good ones that gave you real grief, because you let yourself care about them. Tsali had been only ten minutes late. Usually Doc's customers were at least an hour late—when they managed to get there on the right day. So the old man let it go.

This was a good kid. A real good one. His dark skin showed he wasn't all white. He looked like some of the mulattoes on the island, those who bore traces of all the various races that had mingled here over the centuries. Every once in a while one of them would come along who seemed to go straight back to one of the groups, seemed almost an archetype of an ancestor who had provided no more than one-sixteenth or one-thirty-second part of his blood. A light-skinned mother and father would produce a baby with skin as black as Doc's, with a nose that told of African warriors and deep magic from the sub-Saharan world. Or perhaps the same parents would pop a baby with translucent white skin, the kind that only the Dutch have, with blue eyes and blond hair. This kid was like that—the perfection of the race that had owned these islands before anyone else came, the Carib Indians, water warriors, cousins to the Cherokee. That was where Tsali came from. The originals, the ones who had the most right . . .

Doc Wilhelm's thoughts broke off. They were nearing their destination, a particularly quiet cove on the north side of the island, five or six miles from New Delft. He'd not brought Tsali here before, but he knew the kid would like it. Away from tourists, with peculiar formations of coral to admire, and strange and splendid fish to wonder at. But Doc Wilhelm hadn't picked it for that reason alone. He had another agenda. He'd heard the meeting being arranged on the dock the night before. Only his Malay was a little rusty, and he wasn't entirely sure that this was the place. The place where the strangers were congregating.

Damn that VanderVolt woman! If she had left them more than a dozen policemen on the island, if she hadn't disbanded their militia and rendered them defenseless . . .

No use, no reason to go on with that. What was done was done. Doc Wilhelm and the others like him would just have to pick up the slack, the way disarmed soldiers had done for centuries. Even when their countries disowned them, they had their duty. Doc Wilhelm didn't know the enemy yet, but there was one. Doc Wilhelm and the others like him had all felt it, they had all known it . . .

Doc Wilhelm had cut the motor just at the entrance of the cove. The boat slipped in silently and came to rest about thirty yards from shore, gently rocking. The old black man smilingly helped Tsali on with his gear. He explained where they were, the depth of the water, the slight dangers: "You run from the barracuda, hey? You run from that bastard. The shark? Here the shark is a baby, you don't go near him, he leave you alone."

Tsali slipped quietly into the water, not falling over backward with an enormous attention-getting splash the way most of them did, but almost stealthily abandoning the boat. After years of giving instruction to an endless stream of tourists dull of mind, awkward of body, and insensitive to everything else, Doc Wilhelm had at last come across one who made it all seem worthwhile. The mute American boy trained as if convinced that tomorrow his life would depend on his skill.

Doc Wilhelm smiled as he watched Tsali's body disappear, the big tanks of oxygen on his back weightless in the calm salt water.

Tsali had stayed down for three quarters of an hour. He frequently checked both his watch and the gauges on the tanks, making sure that he had air left. He alternately played and worked below the surface of the water. Worked first: doing maneuvers near the bottom in as small a space and as quickly as possible. Pretending he was pursued, and finding a hiding place, experimenting with disguising the bubbles. Deliberately seeking out dark, tiny caverns in an attempt to overcome the slight nauseous claustrophobia he suffered in such places. Just sitting as still as possible, and trying to *sense* the strange, underwater environment.

He played too. Rode on the back of an ancient sea turtle, whose shell was still warm from the sun. Filled the bag that Doc

Wilhelm had given him with small treasures—pieces of coral, unexpectedly blue rocks, exquisite pink shells.

When he found the real prize, he nearly lost his mouthpiece in his excitement. While digging up a small outcropping of coral, he had uncovered a gold coin. Those, Doc Wilhelm had said, were the real things. Things that museums wanted, that people paid lots of money for. It was an old one, too, not perfectly round, but only crudely circular.

Holding the coin tightly in his hand, Tsali swam to the surface. He wanted to show Doc Wilhelm immediately! As he ascended, Tsali thought of all the possibilities. It could have been Spanish, Portuguese, Dutch, Swedish, English—any one of a number of empires that had come and gone, or merely traded, in the Caribbean. Right now the coin was too encrusted for him to read the legend. But Doc Wilhelm would know how . . .

The sun was shining brightly, and the hull of Doc Wilhelm's boat cast a shadowed shaft of darkness through the blue cove water. Tsali broke the surface a few yards from the boat and threw off the mouthpiece. It was times like these—the rare occasions when he was totally happy—that Tsali most regretted his inability to speak. That he couldn't yell for joy. He swam quickly to the side of the boat, and slammed his open palm against the wooden surface—his signal to Doc Wilhelm. Tsali waited, bobbing excitedly in the water.

A moment later all Tsali's excitement ebbed away, without his knowing why. He stopped bobbing and was quiet. He replaced his mouthpiece, and sank quietly below the surface of the water. He knocked quietly in several places on the underside of the boat. He waited several minutes for a response. None came. Tsali cautiously lifted his head above the surface of the water. He removed his goggles, and looked all around. The arms of the cove were rocky, with a few trees precariously gripping among the boulders. The beach was of pure white sand, and beyond it, the forest was a density of black-green vegetation. Tsali saw footprints on the shore—many of them.

Tsali quietly turned the boat so that its starboard side was toward the shore. Then he climbed quickly over the port rail, not even hesitating when he saw that his fear was realized in the worst possible way.

Tsali had seen death. He had even caused it, more than once. But death was always a shock, always a new thing. It was a horror that didn't easily diminish itself in the mind.

A knife was embedded in the back of Doc Wilhelm's head, just below the skull. A few inches of the protruding blade gleamed in the sunlight. Doc Wilhelm lay on the deck of the boat, his head propped on a coil of rope, his last pillow. His eyes were open. Drying blood welled out of his slack mouth, and was drying a dark brown on the coils of rope. There was the stink of shit around him, for the old man's bowels had given way in the attack. Death's final insult.

10

There wasn't time for mourning. There wasn't even time for fear. Tsali knew that those who had come for Doc might come back for him, but he also knew that a warrior never leaves a fellow warrior alone on the battlefield. At all costs, retrieve the body of a comrade, or at least make sure that he is honored in his death. Tsali quickly went over his options. He remembered another thing now, something he had read about in school.

He went carefully down the length of the boat to where the small outboard engine was attached to the hull. Beside it was the expected container of gasoline. Tsali, quite beyond tears but feeling very tired, returned with the can back to Doc's body. He withdrew the knife from Doc's head, and closed the old man's eyes. He folded his rictused hands across his breast. He recalled in his mind the prayer to the fallen hero that the Cherokee speak on the battlefield. He signed it quietly and quickly over the warrior's corpse. Then he stood back and sloshed the gasoline over the body, making sure to soak the clothing and the rope beneath Doc Wilhelm's head.

With the knife that had killed Doc Wilhelm, Tsali severed

the anchor rope. With the tide going on swiftly, the boat began drifting immediately toward the sea. Tsali found a book of matches in the emergency kit.

One last time he scanned the rocks and the beach around the quiet cove. Nothing. No one. Then, with a single motion, Tsali took a single match and tossed it toward the gasoline-soaked corpse. He dived into the waiting sea.

When he surfaced at the left-hand arm of the cove, among the rocks there, the prow of the boat was in flame. It was drifting out to sea, carrying the corpse of a warrior toward the edge of the earth. Just as the Vikings had done, the way Tsali had seen it in the books about ancient worlds. All Tsali had really known was that Doc Wilhelm was a man of the sea, and the Viking ritual of allowing a man's spirit to soar through flames on the surface of the ocean seemed right to him.

The burning boat slipped out between the rocky arms of the cove. A few moments later there was a loud explosion, a *whooosh* of sound as the gasoline in the motor exploded. Then another, louder one, *baaam*, that Tsali thought must have been the oxygen left in the breathing tanks he had abandoned. The sea was littered with the detritus, but a fragment of the boat's hull, still burning, continued its solemn way.

Tsali watched, hidden among the rocks. Watched for the last of the burning, seaborne pyre that was his tribute to the spirit of Doc Wilhelm. He tried to picture the black man's soul elevated to the waiting gods. His memory, Tsali vowed, would remain here on earth as long as Tsali himself lived. Good men are hard to find, Billy Leaps had told Tsali, and when you find them, you capture their spirit and hold it close to your own heart—always.

I will do that, Doc Wilhelm.

Tsali turned in the water, and with slow, deliberate strokes swam toward the shore.

For a warrior, unexpected death isn't a cause for hysteria, for unleashed emotions. Unexpected death, even a friend's, is a signal to attend to the business of war. The enemy has struck—this was the message that Tsali had received.

He would never know—nor did he ever pause to speculate—whether this reaction came to him because he was a Cherokee, because the blood of the most feared of the Indian nations ran in his veins, or because he had become Beeker's son, the chosen offspring of a professional warrior, or simply because he had truly become a member of the team in this moment.

Clad only in his bathing trunks, Tsali walked up the sand of the beach, the white soft sand that tourist brochures proclaimed the most beautiful in the Western Hemisphere. But Tsali wasn't thinking about sand or tourists or promotional brochures. He was looking, watching for an enemy, thinking about balance and cover, moving for the shadows. He carried the knife with which his friend had been killed. Even that knife had spirit to it—the vengeful spirit of a cocked and unsprung trigger. In Tsali's hand, it wanted recompense for Doc Wilhelm's death.

He ignored the well-trod paths. Instinctively, just as naturally as the ancestors that he shared with Beeker would have done, Tsali went directly into the underbrush. Crouched over, running quickly and ignoring the pain of the cuts on his bare feet, he moved silently through the dense tropical foliage.

He was moving, moving fast and silent through the jungle of New Neuzen, waiting for the enemy.

On alert, at an emotional and physical peak his father had prepared him for, Tsali arrived at a clearing. That the short cropped grass belonged to a golf course made no difference to him. He was waiting for an enemy to show himself. And because of that, the sight that greeted him here wasn't unexpected, not at all. He could almost have predicted it. A warrior, especially a warrior forewarned, would never have seen this golf course simply as a posh playground. He would have viewed it as the perfect place for an ambush. And that's just what it had been, the scene of more death. Death unanticipated and undeserved.

Four corpses. Two white, and two mulatto. Tsali moved toward them stealthily. The sickly sweet rot of the forest vegetation was gradually overcome by the stronger, strident odor of human death. More blood, more feces, spilled out on the grass that had been mown that morning. And in the midst of it all, Tsali even thought he could smell the residue of fear—the fear that was still etched in the surprised faces of these four dead men. Two golfers and their native caddies.

The two golfers he recognized from the hotel. One of them he even knew by name. Mr. Dandridge. Amanda Dandridge's husband. Jocelyn Dandridge's father.

Tsali paused. He had spent the night in Jocelyn's room at the hotel. He had left her asleep and gone directly to the pier for his lesson from Doc Wilhelm. If Jocelyn took her breakfast on the balcony outside her room, as she had told him she did every morning, then the trade wind blowing over New Neuzen would spoil her appetite with the stink of her father's murder.

Tsali studied the four gracelessly sprawled bodies. More knives, but this time the knives had been taken away. These corpses were the footprints of the enemy. An enemy that found its foe in old warriors like Doc Wilhelm and unarmed civilians like Mr. Dandridge and his party. Tsali respected the enemy, for a warrior always respects those who bring death—but at the same time Tsali despised their cowardly souls.

Tsali moved back to the cover of the foliage. His hand was kept loosely on the handle of the knife, his only weapon. He pushed through the undergrowth, ignoring the scratches on his back and arms, denying the pain in his feet.

He kept on going. He was near the hotel, and could see it beyond just a few more staggered clumps of vast trees. But something made him suddenly even more cautious. A noise, a strangled cry, like that of a chicken caught by something that would kill it in a few moments.

He crept up to the nearest stand of trees, slipped within their shade, hid behind their wide, moss-shaggy trunks. In the midst of the trees was a small clearing, and the men he saw there were the enemy. Tsali knew it absolutely.

He counted eight of them, ranged around something on the ground. And there, across the clearing, a single black man was tied to the trunk of another tree. He watched the men with the indifference of the insane. His jaw lolled.

When one of the men in the ring suddenly detached himself, Tsali's stomach nearly boiled over. He saw the thin haunches of a ninth man rising and falling over what was apparently a woman—or had been. She was naked, splotched with blood and mud and was actually green from where she'd been crushed in the grass. The men standing around urged their comrade on with words that Tsali couldn't understand, but whose bravado wanted no translating.

It was the woman on the ground who gave off the little cries he had heard. Her breath and her voice came and went. She was long past articulate speech. Tsali had not seen much death, but what little he had seen had all been quick and violent. This was slow and violent. He knew the woman was dying. Tsali was frightened and disgusted. With an overstated final thrust and overacted bellow of conquest, the man arched his body theatrically to announce his orgasm. The man rose and shambled off.

The woman had perhaps five seconds of respite, but she made no movement of protest at all, except to try to turn on her side in the grass. One of the men kicked her onto her back again with the point of his boot. Tsali moved to another tree. The woman's legs were helplessly spread apart. Blood oozed from that secret place he had thought so beautiful on Ruth and Jocelyn. This unfortunate woman's head lolled to the right, and blood seeped from her mouth onto the grass. Her chest heaved, but not in any discernible rhythm.

Tsali felt for Doc Wilhelm's knife. If he showed himself, he'd die. But at that moment, he wanted to sacrifice himself. Not just to kill one of these nine attackers, but to spare the woman even a few seconds of this degradation and pain. To kill her purely as a mercy.

Tsali readied himself to throw the knife, and was waiting only for the surrounding circle to draw apart for a few seconds. When he did throw, he'd run, though he had little hope of escaping all nine men. Then, with a shiver of horror, Tsali saw that his sacrifice would not be necessary. One of the men knelt down beside the woman, and taking a knife from a sheath on his belt, he opened the woman's throat with one quick slash. The face of the man on top of her was drenched in the blood, and he seemed angry at being denied his fun. She was still. Dead.

Tsali closed his eyes at this evidence of what men could be and do. He vowed he'd never be this sort of animal. When he looked up again he saw the blood-drenched man pull up off the dead woman. Tsali vowed he would destroy these animals. One man shambled over to the black man who had been tied to the tree. Tsali realized then that this captive, who had been forced to watch the whole scene, had been the dead woman's husband. Then without warning, the man took out a knife and unceremoniously slit the black man's throat, pushing his head aside quickly so that the blood spouted over the grass.

A dark silent shadow in that noonday world, Tsali crept back to the hotel. To tell Cowboy what had happened. And turn his big brother into a warrior.

11

Tsali slipped quietly in through the slightly opened window of the hotel bedroom. But for the purpose of rousing Cowboy, he might as well have come in with guns blazing, for in an instant Sherwood Hatcher was out of the bed and poised to return whatever attack might present itself. All the daydreams of sex with Amanda vaporized. All the lingering effects of the previous night's booze were obliterated. The primal part of Sherwood Hatcher that was a warrior and made him a natural member of the Black Berets rushed to the fore.

"Tsali!" Cowboy didn't relax even when he realized it was the kid. First, there was the look of determination on Tsali's face. Cowboy had seen that same look before—on Beeker. And the cuts on Tsali's body, each of them a line of glistening blood, showed that he had just been through *something*.

Cowboy in that split second also noted that Tsali suddenly seemed much older—once again years had been added. Or was it that years had been ripped away? That a few hundred more days of his ebbing adolescence had been stripped off. Whatever it was that had happened, Cowboy knew that the boy had been hurtled further toward the goal of his life. He was that much nearer becoming one of the Black Berets in body, in soul, and in experience.

Tsali's hand moved with perfect calibration. While Cowboy dressed, automatically donning the vacation khakis he had brought that were closest to jungle fatigues, he watched the boy's fingers. They went precisely fast enough to tell the story as quickly as Cowboy could grasp it. Tsali seemed to have a perfect measure of Cowboy's ability to follow sign language.

Cowboy thought over the implications. Part of him wanted to get off New Neuzen as soon as possible. Tsali was his responsibility, and already the boy had been put in danger. If he had been on the boat when Doc Wilhelm was attacked . . . Cowboy didn't want even to imagine Beeker's response to such news. But a part of Cowboy—the larger part, he had to confess—wanted to stay on the island. There was action here. And no member of the Black Berets had ever tried to flee the scene of real action. Yet nothing could or should be decided without more information.

"I'm calling home. Got to see if they know anything."

Tsali nodded his approval. If the murders had been a random act—a set of random acts—of violence, it would be one thing. But now, after the past few escapades of the Black Berets, Cowboy had at least to check out the possibility that it all had something to do with them. In certain circles, the Berets had already established a name for themselves. Someone, some organization, might have felt it prudent to eliminate them without further parlay.

Cowboy punched the numbers into the hotel phone. He waited impatiently while the connections were being made.

No answer in Shreveport.

Cowboy slammed down the phone. "Damn it! I didn't bring the equipment!" Cowboy referred to a whole setup of telephonic word processing equipment that he had devised, allowing them to communicate with the home base from any point in the world. It was primarily to keep in touch with mute Tsali when they were away, and to allow important messages to be transferred through him—but Tsali was with Cowboy, and they were on vacation, so Cowboy had left the equipment back in Louisiana. He had packed extra shirts instead.

"Okay, we're gonna see what this shit is all by ourselves." Cowboy took a revolver from his suitcase. "I got another, kid, or you want to stick to your knife?"

Tsali held on to the knife.

"You want to take care of those cuts?"

Tsali shook his head.

"Then put on some clothes, and let's get started."

Tsali indicated that he was ready to go as he was, barefoot, bleeding, wearing only swim trunks and a sheath for the knife.

Cowboy's face was stern then, and his voice full of angry command. "Don't give me any of this hero-Indian shit, boy. Clean up and put on some fucking dark clothes. This is a job and you got to do it right, so put on some shoes too. I don't care how good your fucking feet are, put on those running shoes."

Tsali hurried to do as Cowboy had commanded. He was momentarily ashamed—he had put pride in the combat readiness of his naked body ahead of the security of their mission. Unforgivable. Still, he didn't apologize or explain. He did what he had been told to do, as quickly as he could. He grimaced as he pulled the shoes over the abrasions on his feet.

Cowboy wore dark trousers and a dark brown T-shirt. Tsali wore just a pair of denim bib overalls. He carried two knives, and now he was glad that his father had insisted he learn to throw with either hand.

The two walked along the open corridor of the hotel's third

floor, then down the enclosed staircase and into the lobby. Tsali wanted to take Cowboy out to the golf course, but Cowboy said quietly, "No. Not yet. I want to make sure everything's all right here."

Everything seemed to be. People were milling around the lobby as they always did at this time. Evidently some plane from the States had arrived recently for there was a short line of vacationers waiting to check in.

Let's go, Tsali signed impatiently.

"No," said Cowboy, and led Tsali over to a couch that was tucked out of the way, in a shadowed corner of the lobby near the entrance of the cocktail lounge. Cowboy sat down, and then motioned for Tsali to sit beside him.

Tsali couldn't understand it—why was Cowboy just sitting there, smiling at the people who passed, those coming out of the bar, or going into it? Cowboy looked as if he hadn't a care in the world.

As if divining the boy's thoughts, Cowboy said in a low voice, "This is reconnoitering, Tsali. Something feels off, and I'm not sure what it is. Do you feel it?"

Tsali shook his head.

"That's because you're not still. Your mind is elsewhere. Be still. Open up a little. For right now, our business is here. It's not out on that golf course. It's not back in that cove with Doc Wilhelm. Right here. This could be the next battleground. And if it is, then you need to know it up and down . . ."

Tsali blushed again. He had thought himself well trained, but he had made another mistake, he realized, in imagining that all conflict took place out of doors. That the lobby of a hotel on an out-of-the-way Caribbean island couldn't also hold danger and surprise. He sat back on the couch, imitating Cowboy, and he let his eyes wander. What did he see? The hotel guests who were lurching through in their dripping bathing suits for an afternoon nap. The nervous guests who were waiting for a decent hour to take the first drink of the day without guilt. The drunken guests who didn't feel guilty for guzzling the first rum-and-tonic before luncheon. The too-friendly staff angling for tips either now or at the end of the guests' stay. The new guests, looking pale, and the guests about to depart, looking burned. But after a few minutes, Tsali felt it too. Something wrong. Something that wasn't what it had been yesterday, something that felt dangerous.

Then, just when Tsali was about to tell Cowboy that he did indeed feel something wrong, Cowboy had his hand on the boy's shoulder and was dragging him up off the couch. Easily, as if they had just decided to return to their room, they went through the door to the enclosed staircase. It was a metal door, with a small window inset with mesh. It could be bolted from the inside, and Cowboy did so. Standing in the shadowed concrete stairwell, he and Tsali peered through the small square of glass into the brightly lighted lobby.

Cowboy said nothing. He only motioned for Tsali to watch.

The boy knew that Cowboy had identified the enemy, and he looked hard, hoping to be able to do so as well. At first he could not, but then he realized he was trying too hard. Again, he let his eyes wander over the lobby, just letting what was there sink in.

Then he understood. It was a group. Only it didn't seem a group at first because they were all there in different guises. One a policeman. One a porter. The third a taxi driver who had helped to bring in bags and now was lingering pointlessly at the cigarette machine. Then two who came in together and evidently were trying to cash a check at the cashier's. More only a minute later.

Something Tsali had seen before but now couldn't place again. Some resemblance or pattern . . .

Cowboy and Tsali exchanged glances. Tsali held up eight fingers. Cowboy glanced through the window. "Here come Nine and Ten."

They weren't an attractive group. Far from it. Cowboy and Tsali had picked them out as comrades not from any superficial resemblance, or common behavior, not from signs passed between, so much as by a subtle—and sometimes not so subtle—emanation of rot from each of them.

Tsali couldn't know, but Cowboy did, that this group of men in their elaborate disguises displayed the worst characteristics of the people of the East Indies. Once a proud series of independent nations and later the crown jewel of the Dutch empire, now one of the most populous nations on the earth, the part of the world known as Indonesia had many beautiful people in it—remnants of proud cultures. The dancers of Bali are world-renowned for their grace and beauty. If there is a place of rest for dead warriors, then those of Sumatra will stand alongside the Viking and the Cherokee.

But years of neglect of their bodies, years of corruption of their systems, had left many East Indians perpetual carriers of nonlethal skin diseases, afflictions that were obvious in these men. Eruptions, discolorations, peelings, were apparent on the backs of their hands, on their necks, on their faces—like signposts pointing to the corruption of their decaying souls. Through the steel door, yards away, Tsali thought he could smell them, smell the rot that disfigured them and set them apart.

Once Tsali had identified them, they seemed to stand out as if they had been painted blue. Their eyes, beady and slinking. Their bodies, thin and untrained. Their flesh, carrying the diseases of an overpopulated tropical sewer. They disgusted the Cherokee youth. Even the tourists seemed to sense something about the men, and drew away whenever one of them came near. If the men stayed long enough without making a move, then the lobby would have emptied out.

But they did make a move. At some prearranged signal that was invisible to Cowboy and Tsali in the stairwell. Pistols, long knives, two unfamiliar SMGs, appeared from under loose shirts, out of deep pockets, unearthed from hidden places in the lobby.

The tourists and the hotel staff looked at the intruders with hopeless incomprehension. The ambush wasn't in the hotel's daily calendar. To the uninitiated, weapons look like theatrical props—which is how most people have seen them. Pistols firing blanks. Knife blades that retract. The great majority of tourists on New Neuzen had probably never seen anyone die by real violence. Even with ten armed men in their midst, waving their weapons threateningly, it didn't seem possible that that was what they were going to be exposed to now.

Then a woman screamed. Not a loud scream. Not a long scream. Just a scream that said, *This is real.* At least that's how everybody else understood it, because all at once the hotel guests and staff bolted, in an attempt to flee the large room.

A New Neuzen policeman stationed outside the hotel ran inside a moment later, but one of the Indonesians stationed beside the door cracked him over the head with the butt of his gun. The policeman wasn't knocked out, but he was staggered, and a second Indonesian took away his pistol, and kicked him over against the wall. Inside the stairwell, Tsali pulled his knife from its sheath, but Cowboy motioned him down.

Some of the guests, those nearest the exits or already in the elevator, managed to flee; but the unluckier ones were herded into the center of the lobby, near the check-in desk. The armed Indonesians formed a semicircle around them. Their rotted, green teeth showed between their sneering lips. One of them, more unctuous than the rest, reached out a slimy hand and lewdly stroked the breasts of a terrified American girl who couldn't have been more than fourteen or fifteen.

That could have been Jocelyn, Tsali thought. He glanced at Cowboy, wondering when the Black Beret would make his move, and also trying to figure out what that move would be.

Cowboy was identifying the leader of the group. Any ten men on a mission had a leader.

He had picked one out, who stood a little taller and a little straighter than the others. Cowboy smiled grimly when this one spoke, in Dutch-accented English: "Friends. You are in the safe protection and custody of the Black Palm."

The startled tourists' eyes grew wide. The man's words only made them more nervous, because they had never even heard of the Black Palm. They would probably have felt better if the Indonesians had announced themselves members of the IRA or the PLO. The IRA and the PLO after all were on the evening news.

The Indonesian leader knocked over a table lamp, smashing it on the floor. Then he stepped up and stood on the table. "You are all very welcome in the new Indonesian homeland of Kota Jutan."

The armed members of the Black Palm shouted, "Kota Jutan! Kota Jutan!" The tourists glanced at one another, more and more worried and nervous. There was a trickle of liquid to be heard when the shouting died down, and the members of the Black Palm began to laugh, and to point at a middle-aged woman, weak with shame, who had been unable to hold her urine for fear.

"What of New Neuzen?" came a voice from the crowd. The voice was filled with contempt for the revolutionaries.

Cowboy shifted a little to see who had spoken. It was the policeman, who was holding a kerchief to his bleeding head. Cowboy nodded approval.

"New Neuzen is a colony of the Dutch," said the leader

scornfully. "New Neuzen is nothing. New Neuzen is a toilet for all the races of the earth. Kota Jutan will be a nation for the proud, for the pure, for the brave people of Indonesia!"

"Kota Jutan!" shouted the followers automatically. "Kota Jutan!"

"Those wishing to fight against the Dutch imperialists will be allowed to stay. Others holding on to the corrupt ways of the old regime of New Neuzen and the black sow VanderVolt will be dealt with as I see fit." The leader grinned a menacing grin at the injured policeman. The policeman absorbed the implied threat with an expression of contempt.

"Kota Jutan!" shouted the leader.

"Kota Jutan!" returned his followers.

The flag-waving was premature, and as it turned out, suicidal. Because that was when the injured policeman made his move. He grabbed toward the Indonesian closest to him. The Indonesian wasn't prepared. Holding a rifle, he thought he was invulnerable to these frightened, sunburned tourists. The policeman grabbed the rifle, and turned it on the leader.

He fired.

But not quickly enough, for another Indonesian had stumbled in the way. The member of the Black Palm inadvertently saved the leader's life by placing his head in the path of the policeman's rifle bullet. At such close range, his skull exploded. On the table behind him, the leader was sprayed with blood and the gray matter of his follower's enfeebled brain.

Another of the Indonesians got a shot off, but it went astray, and luckily embedded itself in the hotel desk rather than in one of the hostages. A second Indonesian flailed with his knife toward the policeman, but only managed to stab the arm of one of the hotel chambermaids. She screamed and kicked the man in his groin.

"Now," said Cowboy quietly in the stairwell. He unbolted the door, and pulled it in toward him. He and Tsali still remained in the shadows. In the lobby all was pandemonium. The circle of Indonesians had been broken, and the guests were trampling out over the body of the dead man. The Black Palm members on the other side were shooting into the crowd, and several persons had already fallen.

Cowboy turned that way first, and in rapid succession, picked off three of them. One in the temple, one in his right eye, one in the heart.

Tsali threw his first knife into the neck of another terrorist who was reaching out with his own knife for the policeman. The knife jarred into his throat, severing his jugular artery. His blood and life spewed out in a great arc over the frantic crowd. He staggered and fell, and for a few moments more, his blood spouted out across the floor.

The leader of the group, seeing that his men were dropping even faster than the tourists, hopped down from the table, and holding his pistol aloft, scurried for the front door of the hotel.

Tsali stepped calmly out of the stairwell into the lobby of the hotel. He turned in that direction, and let fly with his second knife—the knife that had killed Doc Wilhelm.

The knife sang through the air, turning end over end, and a quarter-second later embedded itself in the back of the leader's neck, slicing upward into the brain. He died as Doc Wilhelm had died.

With the fingers of his knife-throwing hand held behind his back, out of sight of anyone else in the room, Tsali quickly signed, *For you, old man.*

12

Roosevelt Boone was bored to tears. He was just beside himself with boredom. *Why?* he kept asking himself. *Why am I bored? Got this nice little cottage right on the Gulf of Mexico. Got me a fine rod and reel. Got me a ripe woman down the path who starts spreading her legs every time she hears my back door slam. Case of cold beer in the fridge. Everything a man could want.*

Except his friends.

It galled Roosevelt Boone no end. You'd think he'd be in pigshit heaven, what with a week off, a week without the whining voice of Marty Applebaum and his outrageous, unceasing bragging. A week without watching Beeker play the Great White Leader—well, Great Half-White Leader. A week without feeling guilty because he hadn't taught Tsali something new in the past twenty-four hours. A week without having to look back into Harry's sad eyes. A week without having to listen to Cowboy's latest plot to sneak in the cocaine or booze that Beeker had denied them . . .

But Rosie missed it all. He'd be sitting out there on the end of the dock, in cut-off jeans and a white T-shirt and a big straw hat like his grandmother used to wear when she went fishing in the Hudson River, waiting for the fish to bite—and he'd start to think about Tsali, and wonder what the kid was doing. He'd want to hear Beeker's latest goddamn plan to make the Black Berets more like the Marines—or what the Marines *should* be. And it started to seem too quiet without Marty's chatter.

On the fourth day he realized with a start that what he was feeling was homesickness.

Homesickness.

Like a six-year-old kid, sleeping away from his parents for the first time.

Rosie grinned at the Gulf of Mexico.

If you were homesick, that meant you had a home.

And knowing he had a home made Rosie feel proud and happy.

He threw his new rod and reel in the Gulf of Mexico, and walked the two miles up the dirt road to the little country store with the pay phone outside. He eagerly punched the number of the Shreveport farm.

Marty answered. "Okay, asshole," growled Rosie—trying to keep the grin out of his voice—"what's going on? What's happening?"

"Rosie! It's an alert! It's this full fucking alert—that's what's going on! Oh, God," whispered Marty, "I just can't fucking believe it, 'cause there's this full fucking alert, and there's nobody here 'cept Harry and me."

"Calm down, you asshole," said Rosie. The black man knew that anything Applebaum said was exaggerated. But Rosie also could detect the edge that came into Marty's voice when the thing was real. And that's what he heard now—that edge of reality.

"It's Cowboy and Tsali," said Marty. "These communist terrorists, there were these fucking fascists and they—"

"Stop!" Rosie commanded. He ran a hand across his forehead beneath the brim of the straw hat. The sun was high in the sky over the little country store on Florida's northern Gulf coast. "Slow down and tell me exactly what's happening. And leave out the communists and the fascists. Just fucking tell me what happened to Cowboy and Tsali." Christ, Cowboy and Tsali are on a vacation in . . .

"New Neuzen," said Marty breathlessly. "There were these terrorists—"

"Are they hurt?" Rosie demanded.

"Don't know yet. So Beeker's on his way down there—"

"What about you and Harry?" said Rosie.

"Shit, Beeker said we had to stay here, and guard some goddamn woman. Makes me so goddamn mad, Rosie! I want to be there when Beeker shows up. It's gonna be great, it's gonna be the start of a whole fucking war. By the time Beeker's done down there we're gonna probably be bombing Sumatra. Beeker said he was gonna blow those fuckers right off the face of the earth if they tried anything with Tsali." There was a sudden drop in Marty's voice. "How's he gonna do that without me? I'm the one who blows things up around here, not him. How's he think he's gonna pull something like that off without me?"

"That's it, Marty!" shouted Rosie. "That's enough. Put Harry on the phone. Just shut your mouth and put Harry on the phone."

"Rosie—"

"*Harry,*" demanded Rosie.

There was silence for a few moments. Rosie didn't even try to make sense of all that Applebaum had said. Then Harry's low, even voice came over the receiver. "Rosie. It's bad." In those few words Harry communicated more information than Applebaum had been able to get across in all his fevered ranting.

"We're talking about New Neuzen?"

"Yeah."

"Tsali and Cowboy are in real trouble?"

"Probably. We haven't heard from them."

"Are you going there?" asked Rosie. "Applebaum said—"

"Yeah, that was right. We're guarding somebody for Beeker." There was no emotion in Harry's voice. Seldom was. Rosie couldn't even remember the last time.

"I'm going," said Rosie. "Catch me the next plane out of this place. Wherever the hell I am," he added, almost to himself, as he looked around the little clearing by the side of the dirt road.

"That's what Beeker said to tell you if you called. Good luck. 'Bye."

And then the line went dead.

Which was worse? Rosie wondered. Applebaum's endless excited chatter or Harry's laconic, distanced matter-of-factness? Didn't make much difference now—Rosie knew all he needed to know. That Cowboy and Tsali were in trouble on New Neuzen, and that Beeker wanted him there to help.

Vacation! He should have known better. But Rosie was honest, and admitted his relief. Fishing wasn't the thrill he'd remembered it.

13

The Indonesians were cowards. They had no compunction about shooting unarmed tourists in the back—five visitors from America lay dead on the floor of the hotel lobby—but once they were fired back upon, they scattered. Some fled through the front doors, others through the bar. One leaped for the stairwell in which Cowboy still hid himself. Cowboy shot him through the neck at point-blank range. Cowboy's grin was as great as the Indonesian's look of surprise.

Of the ten members of the Black Palm who had invaded the hotel, only four escaped. That quartette wouldn't have made it to safety had there not been such a frantic crowd of bystanders and hostages to make picking them off impossible for Tsali, Cowboy, and the New Neuzen policeman.

One of the hostages in the lobby was a doctor. She began treating the wounded immediately—while most people around her were still screaming. And to the hotel manager, she briskly pointed out those who were now beyond her help. He and two chambermaids dragged the corpses into the hotel office.

The lobby had emptied out for the most part. The doctor

and her patients remained, the patients spread out on the couches and sprawled in the chairs. One Canadian woman stood dazed at the pay phone, and repeatedly dropped coins into the machine though the manager had already announced that all the telephones were dead. Cowboy, Tsali, and the New Neuzen policeman alone stood calm and still. Cowboy held out his hand and introduced himself.

"Jan van Waring," the policeman returned, shaking Cowboy's hand. The name sounded strange coming from a black man, but there were also bright blue eyes shining out of the brown-skinned skull.

"You and I have some work to do," said Cowboy, and the policeman nodded.

Tsali moved forward a step.

"This is Tsali," said Cowboy. "Tsali Beeker."

I will help, Tsali signed.

Cowboy shook his head no. "You have some special business to attend to . . ."

Tsali went to Jocelyn's room and knocked on the door.

"Who's there?" Jocelyn's voice cried out in immediate alarm.

Tsali of course couldn't answer. He knocked again, hoping she'd understand.

The door opened a crack on its chain. When Jocelyn saw it was Tsali, she quickly unchained the door and let him in. She stared at him tremulously for a moment, then threw her arms around his neck.

"We heard shooting downstairs . . ." she whispered. "And my father hasn't come back. We're . . ."

The room was in total disorder. Jocelyn's suitcases were opened on the unmade bed, and all her clothes thrown atop them. She was simply stuffing them in as quickly as she could.

The door to the adjoining room was open, and Tsali saw that it was in a similar state. Amanda Dandridge moved about nervously, also packing, for herself and her husband.

Amanda Dandridge saw Tsali, and came into the room.

"Is Mr. Hatcher . . ." She didn't finish the sentence. "My husband . . ." she began, then couldn't finish that one either.

Both women looked at Tsali as if hoping he would explain what was happening in this beautiful place that had so suddenly turned ugly. Gunshots and screams. Not what you expected to hear at noontime in New Neuzen's most expensive hotel.

No, thought Tsali, *they don't want me to explain what happened. They want me to tell them that everything's all right.*

But everything wasn't all right. By now the flies were swarming over Mr. Dandridge's body. In this heat and high humidity the body would already have begun to turn black on the sward of neatly trimmed grass.

Tsali was uncomfortable. He hadn't wanted to come at all. It hadn't occurred to him as necessary. But Cowboy had told him what to do, and now he was here, intending to do it.

He looked at Jocelyn, frightened. Last night—was it only last night?—he had allowed her to play out some little mothering game with him just so he could prove himself a stud by sticking his thing up her three times in the course of the night. He had slept in this unmade bed. He had used and discarded her, and had never expected anything more to pass between them—certainly nothing of importance. But now he found that she truly needed his support and assistance.

He went to the desk, and took out a sheaf of hotel stationery and a pen. He wrote on the first sheet, "*I'm sorry. Mr. Dandridge is dead.*"

Jocelyn had been reading over his shoulder. She screamed, and fell back.

Amanda Dandridge rushed forward and snatched away the page, read it, stared at Tsali, and said quietly, "Are you sure? Are you absolutely certain?"

Tsali nodded.

"Did Mr. Hatcher send you?" she asked.

Tsali nodded again. He looked over at Jocelyn. She was staggering toward the windows. Her breath came in heaving sobs.

"Was he . . ." the stepmother began, but broke off. "Was it downstairs?" she asked after a moment.

Tsali shook his head. He wrote on a second sheet of paper, "*Danger. You must go. I will help you.*"

Amanda Dandridge blinked away the tears that had formed in her eyes. She looked at Tsali. "Do we have time to pack?"

Tsali shook his head, no.

Amanda turned to her stepdaughter and said quickly, sharply, "Get your purse and your money, Jocelyn. We have to get out of here."

"No! Father—"

"There's nothing we can do," said Amanda. "Mr. Hatcher will make sure that everything's taken care of, won't he?" she asked Tsali. Tsali nodded, yes.

Jocelyn turned back with tears in her eyes, and still shook her head, no.

Amanda Dandridge ran into the next room, and gathered up her purse, money, and credit cards. In a moment she came back, and finding that Jocelyn hadn't moved, did the same for her stepdaughter.

"We're ready," said Amanda Dandridge. "Tell us what to do."

Tsali respected Mrs. Dandridge. He didn't think she was being callous in thus fleeing the place where her husband had been killed. Tsali had been trained in the ways of self-preservation—and that's what this woman was showing. An instinct to stay alive, even if that meant letting the dead lie where they had fallen.

Tsali put a firm arm around Jocelyn's shoulders and led her out of the room into the corridor. The three went to the stairs, and walked down. Tsali in the lead, Mrs. Dandridge in the rear, pushing sobbing Jocelyn ahead of her. They went through the lobby as quickly as possible, the two women staring at the injured still on the couches—one of them with a bloodstained sheet draped over.

"Is Father—" began Jocelyn.

Tsali shook his head, no. Her father was not here.

Tsali knew the Dandridges had rented a car during their stay, and he took the keys from Mrs. Dandridge. With the two women crouched on the floor in the back of the automobile, Tsali drove to the airport. Leaving the two women hidden in the car, he reconnoitered the small facility for the presence of any of the men he now knew he could recognize as Indonesians. He saw none, but he noted that many of the ticket clerks and airline personnel looked nervous—he conjectured they'd already heard of the attack at the hotel.

Tsali hurried back to the car, and got Amanda and Jocelyn Dandridge out. He brought them inside, and handed them a note which read simply, "*Take the first plane out.*"

Jocelyn hung on Tsali's neck. Amanda Dandridge walked up to the ticket booth for Eastern Airlines and, with a smile that was only slightly nervous, asked, "What's the next flight leaving here?"

Following Cowboy's instructions, Tsali saw the two women onto the plane, and he saw the plane take off. He was sad. This adult thing had got very serious all of a sudden. But he knew that he wasn't going to run from it, any more than he had run from the corpse of his new friend, Doc Wilhelm.

He was relieved when the plane disappeared from view. It

was one thing to take care of himself, quite another to bear the responsibility for the safety of two women who knew nothing of violence or of how to protect themselves.

He returned to the terminal, and saw two of the Indonesians there. One coming out of the men's room. One standing idly beside a vending machine. Tsali had his knife, but he couldn't do anything here. It would have been difficult to explain to anybody but Cowboy why he had simply walked up to two inoffensive dark-skinned men, and plunged a knife up under their ribs to spear their hearts at the tip of its blade.

Tsali felt frustrated. He knew that Cowboy was out with Jan van Waring reconnoitering the island for other terrorist activities. He had admonished Tsali to return to the hotel after he had seen Amanda and Jocelyn Dandridge to safety. But instead of that, Tsali drove the rented car north, as near as he could determine, in the direction of the cove where Doc Wilhelm had lost his life. When the roads narrowed, turned from pavement into dirt, and finally petered out altogether, Tsali got out and slipped into the dense underbrush.

Tsali had just figured out why Doc Wilhelm died. Jan van Waring had mentioned to Cowboy that after the disbanding of the New Neuzen military, a kind of shadow national guard had been set up to protect the island in case of attack. Surely Doc Wilhelm would have been part of such an organization, and the terrorists would have gladly murdered any member of that underground security force.

Avenging the death of his teacher and friend was added to the list of Tsali's responsibilities. The cove had to have answers, he decided. And if not answers, then at least clues.

Tsali walked in a straight line till he got to the shore. Then remembering that he had passed this stretch of beach earlier in the morning in Doc's boat, he simply walked northward, always staying within the protecting line of trees, until he came back to the cove. He shucked his clothing, leaving only his bathing suit and the knife in its sheath. He swam out along the left-hand arm of the cove. It was low tide, and the rocks were covered with a slimy green weed. Remembering Cowboy's lesson from the hotel lobby that morning, he did not actively explore the cove at first. He merely hid himself among the boulders and gently bobbed up and down in the gentle waves. He watched.

His watching was rewarded.

A group of the Indonesians appeared on the shore, bringing with them a small green boat which they immediately launched. Laughing and chattering in Malay, they paddled out into the cove. They would have come right by Tsali, but before they got that far out, they suddenly turned to the right, and headed straight for the rocks that made up the right-hand arm of the cove. These were higher and steeper than those on the left-hand side, where Tsali was hidden, and the Cherokee youth wondered what the Indonesians were up to.

Then quite suddenly, a moment after they had fallen within the shadow of the rocks, they ducked their heads and disappeared. Indonesians, boat, and all.

Tsali still could hear the echo of the laughter, however.

It was a cave obviously, with an entrance that appeared only at low tide.

Tsali scrambled up on the rocks, and prepared to dive in on the other side. He'd assault enemy headquarters by himself. Or at least return to Cowboy with a detailed description of the Indonesians' hiding place.

But the boulders exposed by the retreating tide were slippery with weed, and Tsali slipped. He fell backward. There was a hard thump on his head, sudden intense pain, and then the bright New Neuzen sunlight was swallowed up in darkness.

14

"Your love of weapons—of death and carnage in general—is an insult to the human race," said Beatrix VanderVolt. It wasn't what she had intended to say to this strange-looking blond man with the thick eyeglasses. But it was what she couldn't help but say, after she'd heard another of his tirades. Every humanitarian principle she held dear was contradicted by Martin Applebaum's words and opinions.

"I *am* an insult to the human race!" Applebaum retorted. He jumped up on the leather couch that had been placed in the farm's living room and pounded his chest in a rather feeble imitation of Tarzan.

Harry sighed deeply. When Marty got in company, Harry spent most of his time apologizing for his friend. "It's just a show, ma'am," he assured the prime minister. "I mean, you know, we fight and all. But we're not *bad* guys. Not like Marty tries to make out."

It wasn't Harry's words that reassured her. It was the calmness in his voice. She looked over at the big man whose eyes had seemed to call out for comfort since the first moment she had looked into them.

That had been only the day before. After the attack on her in the New Neuzen embassy, Delilah and Mr. Beeker had driven her to Delilah's home in Virginia. There Beatrix VanderVolt had read all Delilah's files on the Black Palm terrorist group. When she closed the last folder, she was more frightened than she had been when she saw a pistol raised and pointed at her in the embassy drawing room. The following morning Mr. Beeker and Delilah had taken her to Dulles International Airport. Beside a chartered plane there she had posed smiling for photographs, and had spoken to a couple of reporters about her intention to visit Louisiana and east Texas on a brief agricultural inspection tour. And a few minutes after that they were in the air and headed for Shreveport. It was at the hot Louisiana airport—not much bigger than the one at New Neuzen—that Beatrix VanderVolt first saw Harry. Standing beside the door of a bright green pickup truck.

"Mr. Pappathanassiou will take care of you," Delilah assured her, as Beeker unceremoniously tossed the prime minister's bag into the rear of the vehicle.

"Call him Harry," said Beeker.

The prime minister shook hands, a little uncertainly. "How do you do, Harry?"

Harry just nodded in return. Leaving her with Delilah, he spoke earnestly for several minutes with Beeker, well out of Beatrix's hearing. When he was done with that, he didn't even wait for Beeker and Delilah's plane to take off again. He simply waved her toward the door of the cab, climbed in himself, and drove off. He spoke to her only twice, once when they'd just left the airport. He said, "You can trust Billy Leaps."

"I know," she said in reply, and meant it.

Then, after they had driven eleven or twelve miles, Harry stopped at the side of the road, walked over to a fence, reached over and fiddled with something. Then he opened a gate a little farther down the road, and they drove through.

"Deactivating the alarm," he explained. And then advised, "Don't pay much attention to Marty, ma'am."

Delilah and Mr. Beeker had been strange enough. These two were much stranger, Beatrix VanderVolt realized. The little man Applebaum had told her an endless stream of stories, one more violent than the last—stories of such carnage she could scarcely credit them. But when Marty saw the disbelief in the prime minister's face, he had appealed to Harry—and Harry had said that Applebaum only told the truth. That first night Beatrix VanderVolt had gone to bed early with a headache.

The prime minister didn't know what to make of any of this—of the assassination attempt, of the unlooked-for intervention of Delilah and Mr. Beeker, of the most peculiar Louisiana farmhouse, and the two men who were constituted as her guardians. She was given a room that was little more than a cubicle, with a hard cotlike bed. It was unadorned but scrupulously clean, and she slept—oddly enough—very well. In the morning she analyzed the feeling. She had felt safe.

The insult to the human race was still standing on the leather couch, rocking back and forth a little, trying to keep his balance. A thought suddenly occurred to him, and he stopped. That did lose him his balance, and he pitched forward. "Harry! Harry!" he cried. "We got to blow up that field, that new acreage. You promised I could use the new fields."

Harry translated for the prime minister. "See, our friend Beeker, he bought some new land. Got the farm up to over four hundred acres by now. But it's all this scrub pine, soft wood that grew up when the whole area burned a few years ago. Won't do anybody any good, so I promised Marty here he could clear it. We were just going to—"

"We're gonna blow that fucker sky high!" Applebaum crowed, grinning toothily at Beatrix.

"Yeah, well," said Harry, still to the prime minister, "we were planning on using some explosives. And Marty thought"—Harry turned his gaze away from Beatrix's deep brown eyes—"Marty thought we could make it into something sort of enjoyable for you."

"For *me!* Explosions?"

"Well, I mean, see, we're gonna lay it all out now, but we won't set 'em off till after it gets dark. Then it'll be sort of like fireworks, you know?"

Beatrix VanderVolt shook her head and wondered anew at the two men. She felt disgust at the little man's bravado, but she was touched by the peculiar thoughtfulness of Harry.

But *explosions?*

Beatrix VanderVolt spent the day reading reports and later relaxing with a novel she had bought at the Dulles airport. How long had it been since she'd had the leisure for a novel? The book wasn't very good, but she relished the luxury. She sat on the front porch of the farmhouse, and every few minutes she'd put her book down and just smell the air. So different from that of New Neuzen, where every breeze smelled of the sea. Here she smelled earth, conifers, and fresh water.

When the two men returned to the house, they were sweating like field hands. She had heard the little blond man from far off, whooping and bragging. Harry, though, was quiet. Always quiet. It was his natural way, she sensed that—but she also sensed in his consistently polite treatment of her an element of distrust.

Why should he distrust her? The question had occurred to her many times during the course of the day. Why should he be so guarded with her? His sadness—so much greater than any she was used to seeing, a sadness that she had once seen on a group of political prisoners, released after nearly two decades of unjust incarceration—was a sadness that she, or any other woman, yearned to relieve him of.

But the reality was that he distrusted her—and all other women, most likely. There was no way to get around that. It hurt Beatrix to think that she was blocked from placing a soothing hand on his brow, from taking his great hand in hers, from caressing his . . . *That must stop.* She sat up straight in the chair as the two men approached the house. She was, after all, the chief of state of the Sovereign Republic of New Neuzen, not some woman sitting at a table in a cocktail lounge, lusting after the last man to walk in the door.

"You are gonna have a show tonight!" Marty exclaimed. "I got enough C-four out there to blow Moscow!"

"It's a kind of plastic explosive, ma'am."

"See," said Marty, running up to the porch, "there's these two kinds. One's loud and quick, not as destructive, but more showy, you know? The other's not so loud, but it goes longer and it really takes care of shit, I mean it *takes care of shit!* So I got the whole thing out there, the whole twenty acres we're clearing, laid with these different kinds of C-four. I did it just for you, so you'd better appreciate it!" Applebaum's skinny chest heaved with grotesque pride.

"What he means is," said Harry, stretching out on one of the concrete steps and leaning his head back against a post for support, "we didn't just lay it out to take care of the trees. Marty's real artistic about it. He'd laid it just so, and what it means is, you have to watch it from right here. Because that's the best angle. Marty figured it all out specially for you. Marty likes to have an audience."

"I used maps," Marty said proudly.

"This is all insanity," said the prime minister. Yesterday, if she had said those words, they would have come out with anger and outrage. Now she spoke almost with amusement.

"This *is* insanity!" Applebaum leaped up on the porch and flung open the door of the house.

Harry remained outside with the prime minister. She hadn't expected that, and she was surprised when after a minute or two, he had still made no move to go away. She tried to open her novel again, but she kept looking over the top of the pages at Harry. She wished he'd go back inside. It was disconcerting to see him like this, so closely. His skin, soaked with perspiration, looked as if it were covered with matted fur. The odor of his body—clean and masculine—was strong and pungent in the Louisiana breeze. This close, his chest seemed massive. She could actually see the sweat vaporizing from his powerful arms.

"Just steaks for supper," he said at last. "Hope that's okay. Don't do much cooking around here when it's just Marty and me. There's these vegetables in the freezer, but I don't know nothing about—"

"I'll help," said the prime minister. How long had it been since she'd cooked? Probably not since she'd read that last novel.

"Ought to get cleaned up. Probably stink," said Harry, rising at last to his feet. He went inside, and Beatrix VanderVolt was left alone on the front porch. The house faced west. The setting sun hadn't quite lowered over the stand of pine in the near distance, and it shone large and golden directly in her eyes.

How strange it was, she thought, to be a prisoner.

Because that's what she was. A prisoner on this farm, for four days. No matter what happened on New Neuzen in that time, she was here, and could do nothing about it.

She tried to feel guilty for the neglect of her country, but that guilt was contrived. She didn't really feel it.

What she felt was a delicious, perverse pleasure in her

imprisonment. Prisoners had no responsibilities. Nobody expected anything of them. As a prisoner, she didn't have to perform, produce, or give carefully considered opinions on any one of a thousand subjects. The prime minister could read a novel, or help to cook supper, or watch fireworks in the evening.

In this rural prison, Beatrix VanderVolt felt really free for the first time in many, many years.

15

Cowboy stood at the entrance of the Carib Beach Hotel. He'd even put on his uniform. Rosie saw that, and it changed the way Rosie looked at him when he got out of the cab with his single satchel.

"That bad?" Rosie asked.

Cowboy nodded once.

Roosevelt Boone paid the driver, and then he looked at Cowboy once more. Didn't matter that they were standing in front of the most expensive hotel on one of the most beautiful islands in the Caribbean. Didn't matter that both men were supposed to be on vacation. Because both men felt it—they were on alert. Their lives would depend on one another.

Bypassing the desk, Cowboy took the black man upstairs. As soon as they reached Cowboy's room, Rosie started stripping off his clothes. He got down to his underwear. Then he tore open the soft-sided luggage and pulled it out. His uniform. He laid it on the floor, spreading it out, smoothing the wrinkles. He had been wearing the boots, and they were already polished. He wiped from them the little dust that had accumulated in the past few hours.

He pulled on the pants first and snapped the web belt closed. Then the shirt was over his arms and being buttoned, top to bottom, then the sleeves. He stepped into the boots and knelt again to tie them tightly, having already stuffed the trouser legs into their leather.

He stood again. Then he pulled the black beret over his head, covering the black surface of his skull. His head had hair sufficient to keep the skin from reflecting, but no more. "I need it shaved," he said. Since Cowboy was the only other person in the room, it might have seemed that it was to him that Rosie spoke. But that wasn't it. Rosie spoke to himself. Before he went into battle his skull was always shaved. It seemed at times to be a need that was almost genetic, a replication of some ancient ceremony of the African tribe that had spawned his ancestors.

"Beeker and Delilah's plane'll be here in twenty minutes," said Cowboy.

"Then we've got twenty minutes," said Rosie, sitting down cross-legged on the floor. "Do it, Cowboy."

"Usually Harry shaves you," said Cowboy hesitantly.

Rosie was still. Cowboy looking on almost thought he could see a kind of inner peace flooding Rosie. "Harry's not here," said Rosie at last, calmly, as if considering the thing already done. "So you do it."

Rosie wouldn't say anything else, and Cowboy knew he'd never get the man up off the motherfucking floor if he didn't shave his goddamn head. Cowboy rummaged through Rosie's things, came up at last with a small leather case. He opened it, and inside found a straight razor and a coiled strop. He unwound the leather strap, and sharpened the razor against it. When he was done, and had tested the edge at a frightening sharpness, he went into the bathroom with the ice pitcher left by room service's last visit. He returned a moment later with hot water.

Cowboy had shaving cream, but he didn't use it on Rosie's head. Rosie didn't like it that way. Rosie wanted to feel the razor. Even if it cut him, Rosie wanted to feel that blade against the skin of his skull, scraping away the stubble of tightly curled hair—and scraping away what little remnants of civilization had stuck to Rosie since the last time the team went into battle.

Cowboy bathed the razor in the hot water. He removed the cap from Rosie's head, and set it carefully aside.

"You call out if I nick you," said Cowboy nervously, but Rosie didn't even bother to reply.

Scrape.

Cowboy had begun at the right temple.

Rosie was at peace. This was a ritual he always gave himself over to completely. It renewed him. It prepared him for whatever would come after. Rosie knew about death, and what's more, he knew that one day death was going to walk across from the other side of the road, and say, "That's it, Rosie. No more." Death always walked across the road, even when you'd dodged him a million times, back and forth, hidden in the trees, crouched in the ditches, set up a hundred thousand diversions. When you were winded, when you were raising your arms in victory, when you had turned your back for five seconds to whistle at a woman—that's when death just up and walked across and said, "No more . . ."

Rosie didn't care about that. Rosie just wanted to make sure that when his time was up, he was wearing his uniform, and his head was smooth.

It was impossible to explain to anybody why he felt that way. But he did. And the other guys in the team knew it. They couldn't explain, but they didn't laugh at it. Once Rosie had sat down cross-legged on the floor, and handed somebody his razor, nobody laughed at Rosie. Not till the last opponent was dead. Not till the bodies were piled up so high along the road-side that death couldn't have seen him without a periscope. Not till Beeker said, "Okay, guys, pack it up . . ."

Scrape. Around the ear.

Funny. It was funny, wasn't it, about Roosevelt Boone and Billy Leaps Beeker. Rosie recalled how they'd met.

It had been in the battle for Khe Sanh. Just the memory of that bloodbath made Rosie's skin crawl. Those assholes who stood behind banks of computers and wall maps of Vietnam with a hundred different colors of pushpins stuck in it had made a pronouncement: Khe Sanh must not fall. Maintenance of the area was vital. Worth the shedding of ten thousand quarts of blood out of three thousand American troops.

They had fought. They had fought against all the odds and in spite of the stupidest officers Rosie had ever come across—and that was saying something. They had fought when lucky enemy mortar shells had blown apart their ammunition dumps. Had fought when waves of Charlies had stormed their positions. Had fought with fear in their souls and hell in their brains and lead in their bellies. Had fought while their best friends' legs and arms and bodies and heads were blown to little pieces that every medic in Vietnam working double shifts couldn't have put back together again.

Scrape. The other temple. Around the other ear.

Rosie had been one of those wounded. When it happened, he was sure he had gone for it. There he was, an Army man, shrapnel in his gut and his legs, lying helpless in the jungle, just waiting for the first Charlie to come along. Stick him with a knife if he had a knife. Blow away his head if he had a gun. And just goddamn kick him to death if he didn't have anything else. Then Rosie looked up, and there was this blue-eyed jarhead. Except his skin was too dark for such blue eyes—that's what

Rosie was thinking. Rosie was also thinking this was the kind of jarhead that had spent all his forming time in his mamma's belly just waiting for the chance to pop out into a suit of Marine dress blues. Except the blue-eyed jarhead wasn't wearing dress blues. He was covered with mud. And he stank worse than Rosie did.

He dragged Rosie away from the enemy fire. Then, when he dared, he lifted Rosie in his arms and carried him like a goddamn baby. Rosie didn't know how far that goddamned jarhead carried him. A thousand miles, probably. Rosie didn't know 'cause all that distance Rosie was dreaming. Dreaming of a helicopter ride to Da Nang. And a bed with honest-to-God sheets. And he was tasting that food in his mouth. Food that had been cooked within Rosie's own lifetime.

And who broke that goddamn dream? Not Charlie. Not Charlie, though there was a million of him back there about a hundred yards away. Not the goddamn blue-eyed jarhead. He was sailing along like that burning jungle was an obstacle course he had set up for himself in his backyard, and run so many times he could do it blindfolded. Nope. It was a goddamned Marine grunt, fresh out of Lejeune, who got freaked.

They were almost safe. Helicopter. Clean sheets. Hot food. And a shot.

A shot from an M-16.

And there was suddenly blood all over Rosie's face. He opened his eyes then, and blinked away the hot salty liquid. And he saw that the jarhead was bleeding on the side of his head. Rosie tried to raise his hand and cover the wound, but Rosie's limbs didn't work right.

"You stupid shit!" the jarhead shouted at the man out of his own platoon who had blown away half his ear.

That was the beginning of Rosie's allegiance to Billy Leaps. Sometime later, all five of them were together, for the first time, over there. And they stayed together till the war ended, until the last helicopter took off from the roof of the American embassy. And afterward, with no more need of their services, and their records and their experiences deprecated and vilified by the country that had ordered their training, they disbanded. They tried to make believe they were ordinary men. Harry had opened a bar in Chicago. Trading on his skills in explosives, Marty joined a demolitions outfit, and moved city to city all over the country. Cowboy started to do small-time smuggling out of South America, and got hooked on his cargo. Billy Leaps taught "physical education" at a boys school in Louisiana. Rosie worked in the Newark morgue, where he belonged, among the dead and the useless.

Till Billy Leaps had brought them together again. Their memories were potent. They were as much a team now as they had been a decade before. Tied to one another. Tied to their identities as warriors in a world that too often tried to pretend there was no need for such men as they. Tied together by what they were—and what they were not.

Scrape. The back of the neck.

"That's it," said Cowboy. "No more."

Rosie stood then, tall, in his uniform, and replaced the black beret over his smooth black scalp. Once more Roosevelt Boone had been converted whole into that image of himself that he loved, that he hated, that he embraced, that he shrank from—made over into a Black Beret.

16

They looked for all the world like the perfect American couple. He was tall, and his good looks were marred only by the ragged tear where his earlobe used to be. Hard to tell exactly what his story was. Maybe a pro football player who'd dropped out and now managed a string of five successful steak-and-beer restaurants. Dressed in an up-to-date tropical suit. Loose collar, no tie, but still uncomfortably confined. Looking impatient while the New Neuzen customs officials made an inspection of their luggage. The attack at the hotel, the deaths of the golfers, and just this morning two rapes of American tourists in a curio shop in New Delft—none of this had yet been made public. But the island was small, and everyone knew without having to hear it on the radio. The customs men were thorough today.

But her they let go by. Her face was starkly white—an unfamiliar hue in the tropics. Her eyes really did sparkle. Enough to get your eyes higher than her body. Narrow waist, almost cinched. Full breasts, voluptuous hips. And the outfit she wore only emphasized all these points. Nothing she could have worn would have disguised that figure entirely.

Beeker chafed at the charade. "Let's get out of here," he growled as the customs inspector with a broad grin for Delilah X'd their luggage.

Delilah smiled up at him with that expression so common to American wives, the one that said, *Poor little boy's having a tantrum*. She followed him as he grabbed the luggage and walked out of the open-air terminal toward the short line of tiny blue taxis.

Her face didn't change in the cab. She listened to the sounds of the island, in order to acclimate herself to the change. The driver humming to the rhythmic music playing on the single New Neuzen radio channel. The sharp blaring of horns from other, equally furious and reckless drivers. The strange birds in the undergrowth on the sides of the narrow road. The waves on the beach when the route veered sharply toward the shore. She snuggled up to Beeker, linking her arm through his. If the driver looked in the backseat, he'd see only an amorous couple. Or a husband sitting ramrod straight, and a wife who was all curves and seductive smiles.

"Most men I know," she said in a low voice, almost directly in his torn ear, "would love to be taken for my husband."

Beeker didn't respond. He stared straight ahead, past the driver's head, at the narrow, winding road, hot and steaming after a brief shower half an hour before.

"You can't be hostile to me," she went on, teasingly. "You'll arouse suspicion. We're the perfect married couple, remember."

"This is exactly how married couples act," said Beeker. "I was married twice, remember. That probably got in the dossier you keep on me, didn't it? This is exactly how it was, the broad telling the guy how to act, when to smile, when to open the door, picking out his clothes for him . . ."

Delilah laughed aloud. "Beeker, you must have had

something else going in those two marriages. Those women must have had something to offer you."

"Nothing I can't buy for a hundred bucks a night," said Beeker grimly.

Delilah sat back against the seat, and inclined her head on Billy Leaps's shoulder. She didn't want to tease him any more. She could see that he was worried. But still she wondered what it must have been like for him—limited to one woman, to one house, confined to a schedule, with a woman who didn't understand him making constant petty demands. To give her money for this. To take her there. To look this way for her. To be polite to her friends. Delilah couldn't even imagine it. Yes she could, though. Because she had seen a lion, a beast of the African savannahs, who killed for his sustenance—she had seen this creature confined in a cage that wasn't twice his own length. And that's what marriage had been for Billy Leaps. *But why had he married twice?*

She looked up at him, sitting there beside her. He didn't return the glance. He still stared straight ahead. And then the answer to the question came to her.

Because he wanted a son.

Her sources had told her that the Carib Beach Hotel on the western coast of New Neuzen was the biggest, best, and most expensive of the hotels on the small island. But with the New Neuzen operators only giving out the information that the telephones were all out of commission for a day or two, there was no way of confirming the presence of Cowboy and Tsali there. No way except to go there.

Beeker grew tenser as they neared that part of the island. She could tell by the way his muscles flexed beneath his clothes that as soon as the cab drew up before the hotel, he was going to bolt out and leave her to deal with the driver, the bags, and the desk. She wasn't going to try to stop him. It wouldn't have done any good anyway—nothing was going to stop Beeker from making certain that his son was all right.

Beeker didn't have to bolt, however. Because even from a distance through the dirty windshield of the taxi, he made out two familiar forms standing almost at attention by the side of the hotel. Two familiar forms in Black Beret uniforms.

"Cowboy and Rosie," he said quietly.

"Is—" Delilah began.

"Tsali's not with them," said Beeker.

The driver was frightened. As he pulled up before the hotel, the two strangely dressed men marched down the steps toward his taxi. He took his foot off the brake and was about to drive on, but the man in the backseat was already out of the automobile, and the woman was saying to him, soothingly, "It's all right, it's all right, just some friends of my husband's, that's all. They were waiting for us."

Ignoring the stares of the few people who were near the entrance of the hotel, Beeker grabbed Rosie and Cowboy and dragged them off onto the lawn, away from everyone.

"Where's Tsali?" he demanded of Cowboy.

"I told him to stay here," said Cowboy. "I told him . . ."

Cowboy was making excuses. He realized that suddenly. But this was combat, and men in combat don't make excuses.

"He's not here. He went off on his own. He's been gone since about thirteen hundred hours," Cowboy said.

"Which way?" demanded Beeker. "Where the fuck—"

"No way of knowing, Beak," said Cowboy. "I was out reconnoitering. I told the kid what to do, and he didn't do it. He didn't follow orders."

Cowboy didn't try to excuse himself—Tsali *was* his

responsibility. He didn't try to convince Beeker that the kid was probably fine and could take care of himself. Although the sky was bright, the lawn green, and lazy tropical music drifted out through the open windows of the hotel bar—they were in combat. And Beeker, their leader, had arrived on the scene. Cowboy was a lieutenant, reporting the situation. And all three men knew just how bad the situation might be.

Tsali wasn't there.

Tsali, who hadn't deliberately disobeyed an order since the moment that Billy Leaps had laid eyes on him, hadn't returned to the hotel when he was commanded to.

The conclusion was inescapable to Cowboy, to Rosie, to Beeker himself. Tsali was injured. Tsali was captured. Or Tsali was already dead.

17

Delilah had seen it before. It didn't mean she was any less impressed by it. Beeker had joined the other two in putting on his uniform. The three of them stood now, ramrod stiff, at peak, on the balcony outside Cowboy's room. It overlooked the Caribbean. Delilah remained inside the room, studying some of the maps of New Neuzen that she had brought with her.

Out on the balcony, Cowboy explained the hotel's layout to the other two. To the back was the beach and the sea—that at least was straightforward. To the north was the golf course where Dandridge and his party had been slaughtered. To the south were formal gardens, and beyond that a series of private vacation homes, large and exclusive. To the east, toward the interior of the island, was the circular driveway, an extensive lawn, and the road to the airport and New Delft. Beyond was dense tropical forest, gradually sloping upward.

Rosie and Beeker nodded.

Cowboy described the hotel itself. Four floors. Flat roof with a waist-high ledge. From there they'd have a fine advantage over attackers coming in from any side. Still, the rooftop was primarily a defensive position, and the Black Berets had no liking for defense. They were most effective when they were in control, the attackers. But until they knew their enemy, had located his stronghold, and determined his strengths and weaknesses, they could not gain the initiative.

Delilah, in the room, could hear most of what the three men said, though some of their speech was drowned out by the surf. But most loudly of all she heard the one question that wasn't spoken aloud. *Where's Tsali?*

A few minutes later there was a knock on the door. Delilah didn't get up, but glanced out at Cowboy. To ask if he were expecting anyone.

"It's Van Waring," said Cowboy, and went to open the door. A moment later, he let in the New Neuzen policeman. A white bandage had been placed over the lump he'd got in the brawl downstairs.

Cowboy introduced Van Waring around the room. He stared for a few moments at Delilah, but his handshake could not have been politer. He did not question her presence.

"Anything we can do about the civilians here?" Beeker wanted to know. "Half the goddamn rooms are full. Even after what happened this morning . . ."

"Buses are coming for them all," said Van Waring. "Those insisting on remaining on New Neuzen will be transferred to smaller hotels in New Delft. Easier to guard the town right now. But we will try to convince them that it would be best to leave the island right now. If Mrs. VanderVolt will stay out of this for a little while . . ."

"She won't interfere," said Delilah confidently.

"Fine," said Beeker impatiently. "That takes care of the tourists. Now, what do you know about the Black Palm that we don't?"

"The attacks—there have been about five small ones so far. Since this morning. They've all been scattered—"

"Show us," said Delilah. Rosie cleared the end of the bed by shoving onto the floor the suitcases containing Delilah's clothes. Delilah unfolded the silk military map, and spread it out. The island formed a lopsided oval, running about twenty-five miles north to south, with the heavier end of the egg at the bottom. Its entire coast, with the exception of the deepwater port of New Delft, and some rocky inlets on the northwestern edge of the island, were the wide, splendid beaches for which New Neuzen was famed. The rest of the island was tropical forest, with some hills in the center and in the north.

"Tell us what happened," said Beeker. "And tell us when it happened."

Van Waring studied the map for a few moments. Then he pointed. "The explosions first, we think. Here in the north. A small dam on this river. Some houses were flooded, in this area here. Then, as near as we can tell, the murders on the golf course—here. Then the hotel. Then the rapes in New Delft. Then, last, here, the explosion that took out our telephones."

Beeker had watched closely. He retraced the progress of the attacks—they started in the north, came southward, then veered back. With only five incidents, of course, and on a small island, it was not possible to draw a firm conclusion, but he did go so far as to say, "Probably here, in this area, right?"

He pointed to the northwestern coast of the island, five or six miles directly north of the Carib Beach Hotel.

Cowboy and Rosie both nodded agreement.

"What's up there?" Beeker asked the policeman.

"Very little. Forest. Shallow coves. Good fishing," he added with deadpan irony.

Rosie and Cowboy smiled grimly. Beeker did not.

"There's no road between the north and the important targets to the south except the one that goes right by the hotel," he pointed out. "Is that right?"

Van Waring confirmed Beeker's conclusion. "They must come by here."

"And if we blow up that road?" Beeker asked.

The policeman stared at the leader of the Black Berets, shocked.

"There's hills here, a river to cross, more hills, and jungle in between, it looks like," Beeker went on. "They're not going to get from the stronghold to New Delft *that* way. So they either go by boat, or they come through here . . ." He pointed to a second map that Delilah had silently laid out—a much more detailed map of the western portion of the island. "Right along the golf course, and through here. They haven't gone by boat yet, so I'm going to assume they're prepared for assault by land but not by water. And we already know they're familiar with the terrain directly north of here—the golfing party."

Van Waring nodded after a moment's consideration. "Yes . . ."

"And when they come through here, we'll be waiting," concluded Beeker. "That's all. It'll be easy—once we blow up the road out front of the hotel."

"Finally there's a use for Applebaum," growled Cowboy. "And he's not here."

Beeker looked at Van Waring. "Our munitions man is back in Louisiana. Do you have somebody—"

"Kielstra," said Van Waring. "He was trained by the Dutch. A good man."

"We need him as soon as possible," said Beeker. "We're—"

"Kielstra is downstairs," said Van Waring, with a proud smile. "Waiting for orders."

The Black Berets exchanged glances. Their faces were expressionless, but each man was thinking the same thing. These men of New Neuzen—a country without a military, with an emasculated police force, without any real tradition of service—were turning up a small host of competence.

Cowboy had already told Beeker of the corps of old soldiers on the island. Men who had fought for the Dutch in Indonesia. Doc Wilhelm, the old man who had taught Tsali to scuba-dive, was one of them. Van Waring was another, and this munitions man waiting for them downstairs was a third. Beeker hoped there'd be a few more.

"Your group," said Beeker to Van Waring, "they have any weapons?"

"We have a cache," said Van Waring, "and Verbeek's father knows where it is—Verbeek was the one your son saw killed. It was old man Verbeek's job to construct a hiding place."

"Then for God's sake," said Beeker, "let's get this man Kielstra up here—or let's go down to him. We've got to get ourselves prepared."

It was more expedient for them all to go downstairs, and after Kielstra. Delilah remained in Cowboy's room, fiddling with a kind of portable computer that had been packed at the bottom of her bag. The goddamn thing didn't even plug in, but Delilah was evidently talking directly to some other goddamn computer in Washington, D.C., with it.

Downstairs, the buses had arrived, and the lobby was filled with angry tourists, demanding to know why they were being moved against their will.

Typical of a lot of Americans, Beeker thought. Didn't want to give up Days Four and Five of their five-day package deal—even though the blood on the couches in the lobby was still damp and smelled. But even in that noisy crowd, Beeker,

Cowboy, and Rosie stood out. Their stern, expressionless, military presence gave real credence to the warning pleas of the New Neuzen police, and the Americans left more quietly after that.

While Van Waring went to fetch Kielstra, Beeker had a few words for the two men under him in this endeavor: "When everything starts, things'll happen quick. But just remember. I need one of 'em alive. Just one of 'em."

He didn't have to explain why. They only needed one to get back Tsali.

They had gone there alone, Beeker and Van Waring. To a little ramshackle cabin about three miles from the hotel. At the end of a track through the forest that wouldn't have passed muster as a road even in the wilds of northwestern Louisiana. Beeker stood silently by as Van Waring spoke quickly in the New Neuzen pidgin to a man who must have been seventy—the father of the man Tsali had seen murdered on the golf course. Beeker was impressed. He was impressed with Van Waring for showing the guy a whole lot of respect. The bright young cop didn't try to bully the old man—he spoke in even tones, not being really apologetic, but deferential. He knew the old man had once been important, and deserved that respect.

The old man's eyes were on Beeker, though. His even, unembarrassed gaze made Billy Leaps shiver a little when he realized just how thoroughly he was being sized up, measured. Old man Verbeek was the guy with the goods, and Beeker needed them bad. Old man Verbeek was just trying to figure out if Beeker deserved them.

Beeker hadn't been judged this way in a long time. He wasn't used to undergoing this kind of evaluation. The only men who had tried in the past few years to gauge his strength were dead. Those who had seen him in action—with the action directed elsewhere—held Beeker in awe. The weird thing for Beeker now was that he felt that the old man had a right to judge. Beeker could tell just by looking at him that old man Verbeek had been places, seen things, done things . . . that he was a Warrior.

For a crazy moment Beeker thought that if he could speak Cherokee to the old man, then Kielstra would understand him. Maybe it was that thought that did it, who would ever know? But right then old man Verbeek waved assent. Then he spoke a few brief pidgin words to Van Waring.

"Let's go," said Van Waring quickly, as if fearful the old man would change his mind. "We're in big luck."

Old man Verbeek led Van Waring and Beeker around in back of his house. A few hundred feet into the underbrush, back where the jungle was stealthily fighting back against the feeble encroachments of civilization, was an even smaller shack. But this one was built of stone. It somehow reminded Beeker of his own place back in Louisiana. One thing was for sure: this place hadn't been built to house garden tools.

Old man Verbeek pulled a key off the ring that hung from his belt and undid the flimsy Yale lock that defended the rickety door. Then he crouched on his arthritic limbs and carefully detached a wire that wasn't visible to Beeker at all till an inch or two of it glinted in the sun.

"A bomb," explained Van Waring unnecessarily. "Just in case . . ."

Beeker had expected that. He made no comment.

The old door creaked open. The three men walked inside. Van Waring swept the area with a flashlight. Beeker saw many stacked crates, each labeled, however, with a single character in red paint. These characters were some sort of code, possibly known only to the old man. But some of the crates bore the original labeling, and Beeker whistled appreciatively. "BARs . . ."

The heavy, brute Browning Automatic Rifles had been the SAWs—the squad automatic weapons—for the United States for years, until usurped by M-14s, M-16s, and Applebaum's beloved, the M-60. The BAR was sturdy, serviceable, reliable . . . and deadly in the hands of the right man.

"Fine for us," said Beeker. "What about your men?" he asked Van Waring.

"We were trained on these weapons," replied Van Waring.

Then the old man spoke briefly, and Van Waring translated: "We will be proud to use them again. Against the invaders."

18

I am forty years old. I am the prime minister of the Republic of New Neuzen. I am a well-educated woman, the chosen leader of my people. I am a respected member of the leadership of the Free World. Three days ago I addressed the General Assembly of the United Nations. My words were translated into two dozen languages.

Beatrix VanderVolt kept saying those words to herself. Over and over again. She had to remember them. She had to, because the presence of Harry threatened to overwhelm her at any moment.

He had showered and dressed in casual clothes whose khaki material made them seem uniformlike. The hair of his body spilled out over the triangular neck of his shirt, black and dense. His trousers still displayed the power of his legs. His odor was no less masculine now that his body had been freshly washed. The scent of shaving cream and soap mingled with it seductively.

Seductively!

The word seemed so strange to Beatrix. She had ceased feeling such things since her husband had died. The widow of the Great Leader, and now head of state herself, she was not treated as a woman by the population of New Neuzen. She had no real friends, male or female. She knew cabinet ministers, secretaries, other world leaders, gardeners at the residence given her by the New Neuzen Assembly. She knew reporters, and judges, and she knew a number of the very rich people who owned mansions on the west coast of New Neuzen. But a man who treated her like a woman?

Not even Harry did that. But with Harry there was a difference. Beatrix VanderVolt wanted him to.

They were sitting at the table finishing their meal. Beatrix had figured out how to carry on a conversation with Harry despite the incessant intrusions of Martin Applebaum. You just pretended that you and Harry were husband and wife, and that Marty was your spoiled, unruly, selfish child. You talked to Harry, and when Marty interrupted, you nodded once to whatever he said, made brief eye contact, and then went back to Harry.

And because this method worked, Beatrix was able to find out more about Harry. The details weren't easy to get out—he released them one by one, and with apparent reluctance. She knew he was from Chicago, that Vietnam was the most important era in his life until the recent founding of the Black Berets under the leadership of Billy Leaps Beeker. And she discovered that he had once been married—but to whom, and under what circumstances, and how it had ended, he would not say. That conversation about marriage was the only time that Harry was overtly rude to her.

"*Forget it!*" His cry was so vehement, so heartfelt, that Beatrix knew it was forbidden territory. She quickly backed off.

The wine was surprisingly good. Beatrix sipped at it. The other two were drinking beer. It seemed likely that both the bottle and the glass she was drinking out of had been bought specially for her. It would be easy to consume the whole bottle, she decided, to abandon the usual reserve she held herself in, then to reach across the table and . . .

Beep . . . beep . . . beep . . .

Marty and Harry jumped from their seats. "Probably just a deer," Harry said.

"Effin' commies!" swore Applebaum, but without apparent rancor. Marty swore at everything like that, the prime minister had discovered.

Both men moved quickly to the back of the house, toward a room whose door Beatrix had never seen open. She followed and found their two faces intently studying a set of amber computer screens. She was momentarily shocked by the apparent sophistication of the equipment in this windowless room. It was more complex, and doubtlessly more expensive, than anything on New Neuzen.

She moved over to see what they were studying. One screen in particular held their attention. "There gotta be at least twenty of 'em. Jesus Christ!" Harry spoke with unusual vehemence.

"More." Marty's voice was the opposite. Calm for once, concentrated. This reversal of their usual manner made Beatrix uneasy. It suggested that whatever bothered them was a serious affair.

"Obviously going frontal," said Harry. "No cute tricks on the side. No pincer movements . . ." He was studying the screen aloud. "Won't be nice," he concluded.

"We can do it," Marty said, but without his usual bravado.

Both men continued to monitor the screen. Then Harry said, "You know where they're headed, don't you?"

"Oh *Jesus*," exclaimed the other man, with a grin. His little eyes bulged behind his spectacles. "Oh Jesus, Harry, can we do it? Can we *really?*"

Harry raised himself erect and turned to the prime minister.

"You nearly got it in Washington. If we don't stop this little group coming this way, you may get it in Louisiana instead. We're gonna try to stop 'em, but we need your help."

"Anything." Beatrix VanderVolt meant it. She had seen the look on her assailants' faces the last time, when Beeker had saved her. She had found out much about the Black Palm in the meantime. And though she hated violence, and loathed the thought that her protection might be the cause of the deaths of others, she had no intention of dying in the perverted cause of this band of outlaw Indonesians. It was one thing to die for a friend, to die for one's country, for an idea, or an ideal—and quite another to perish at the hands of a perverted, shameless, criminal tribe of Asian degenerates.

Harry led the prime minister back to the large living area. A moment later Marty appeared again, carrying a small portable console, about the size of a typewriter keyboard, but with two rows of switches instead of keys.

"The charges are set to go," he said quickly. "Hooked up to electronic detonators. One for each switch, except these last two over here. You don't have to worry about them," he grinned. "They don't blow up anything. When you get the signal, just flip the switches. Fast as you can, any order. But it'll be neater if you work from both sides in toward the middle. Got it?"

"What's the signal?" she asked.

"A yellow flare," said Harry. "You know what that is?"

"Yes." She'd seen them in Dutch NATO war games, fires that streaked brightly colored paths through the night air.

"We're going out, one of us on each side of the little visiting party. We're going to do a couple of maneuvers, like flank attacks, except there's only one of each of us. We're gonna hope they don't know that."

Beatrix VanderVolt stared. It was scarcely two minutes since they'd heard the alarm. And in that time, an entire plan of attack had been formulated and set up. As far as she could see, there had been no consultation between Harry and Marty. She was awed by their ability to work together in perfect synchrony on something like this.

"What we're gonna try to do," said Marty, "is push these guys in together, real close. Maybe back 'em up a little bit, and get 'em to go where we want 'em to be. So all you have to do—"

"Is sit out on the porch," Harry went on, taking up Marty's instructions seamlessly, "and when you see the flare, start pulling the switches."

Then Marty, with expanded cheeks, gleefully imitated a whole series of explosions.

How deceptively quiet it is.

At first Beatrix was sure she meant the night. The evening was still. Small animals and insects made the pleasant and surreptitious noises close to the house. Even directly underneath the porch where she sat a cricket chirped incessantly. The sky was brilliantly clear. The stars shone in the crisp air. When she looked up, she could count all seven sisters of the Pleiades.

But the night and the stars weren't what was so absurdly quiet. She had been thinking about the thing on her lap. The little metal board with two dozen switches on it.

She thought of every ethical debate on war she had ever heard. She remembered her own speeches in the tiny New Neuzen Assembly. Like the original English settlers of New England, she had wanted to create a City on the Hill, a place of such good and peace that the world would be forced to acknowledge and follow its example. Their moral authority and superiority would lead the way to a New Jerusalem.

New Neuzen had disarmed. Beatrix VanderVolt had stripped

her country of its defenses, confident that the world would never allow it to be seriously endangered. But now her country was in mortal danger. So was she. And in her lap was the means to protect herself. So she might live to protect her beleaguered island in turn. In her lap was the machine that could save her life and the freedom of her people.

The decision to use the machine frightened her. No, that wasn't quite it. What frightened her was the ease with which she had made the decision to put her own safety above the lives of the twenty men who had come to kill her. She scanned the sky, waiting for Harry's yellow signal.

She was momentarily filled with self-hatred. What a coward she was. Oh yes, perfectly willing now to pull switches to kill men from a distance, at night, when to her they were no more than twenty tiny triangles on an amber screen. Utterly capable of making such a decision as *that*. But how different from those two strange men, the Black Berets, the ones who would move in close, and see skulls bursting open, blood flowing like a spring flood, internal organs splashing against trees, severed legs bouncing on the ground, privates reduced to bloody dripping mush.

And what if Harry and Marty walked into that area of death? What if they were fooled or outflanked or mistook their own boundaries? What if they were themselves exposed to the deadly charges with which she would fill the air? What if the yellow flare signaled their own deaths? How much braver they were than she!

She was like the pilot of a B-52 in Vietnam who studied a screen and, with only the aid of a computer to calculate the rotation of the earth, pushed buttons that sent burning death down on faces that would never recur in nightmares, because they had never been seen in the first place. She was like a pilot who would never return, on the ground, to the scene of his devastation. Never count the smoking pots on the Buddhist burial ground. Never see the farmer's plow turn up the shattered bones. Never look on the heaps of skulls and regret the flesh that an act of hers had blistered and burned.

She suddenly thought she understood something of Harry's intense sadness. How often must he have done this? How often must he have killed, and seen the face of his victim? What dead men crowded his sleep? What wounds did he vainly attempt to heal in his dreams? What agonies did he fail to alleviate, night after night, on that narrow cot in his unadorned room?

Beatrix's fingers itched to be at the switches. Now! Kill the bastards who would put her in such a position! Who planned such devilment against her country! Blow apart the bastards who would bring this psychic hell into every moment of Harry's life.

The loud and unmistakable retort of rifle fire filled the night. Beatrix was startled. The noise of war! Sudden and unmistakable. She had never heard it except in the little games the Dutch troops had played with blanks and tracers. The sudden movement of her surprise sent the control panel sliding off her lap and crashing to the porch floor.

She studied it with shocked dismay. *What if I broke it?* Those two warriors had gone into the field asking her to accomplish a simple thing, a single act in their shared defense. What if her bungling created death for them all?

Reverently, prayerfully, she bent and picked up the console. She replaced it on her lap with care. It had fortunately fallen right side up, not with the switches down. *Please, whatever god sees these things, let it still work. Please let it work!*

Her face was frozen with the shock of what she might have done. She studied the horizon. Waiting. *This is what they must go through.* Being responsible for the ambush, creating the diversion, waiting for the moment that would prove them right or wrong. *If I have created their death . . .*

The flares were brilliantly yellow as they carved their way into the sky. One from either side. Their paths crossed elegantly directly before her. *How beautiful,* she thought. But even then she was pulling the switches, from the outside in, just as Marty had told her.

And with the very first switch there was an answer.

BOOOOOM!

Then one after the other, overlapping as her fingers had overlapped. She watched in awe. The whole sky before her was lighted up, orange and yellow, great arcs of colored destruction. And little black silhouettes, like clever paper cutouts, against the orange and yellow—of tree trunks, and branches, and men's legs, and men's trunks, and men's arms still clutching their useless stick rifles.

And what was most appalling, the prime minister thought, was that the scene really did have a kind of structure and rhythm, like a good fireworks display. High blasts and low blasts. Orange blasts with a hint of red. And yellow blasts with a hint of blue. A blast on one side countered by a blast on the other, and a third blast, in the middle, overpowering them both.

An artist! Martin Applebaum, in his thick glasses, was an artist with explosions. *A Michelangelo of death. A Leonardo of destruction. An artist!*

19

Rosie was leading Cowboy around the perimeter of the grounds of the Carib Beach Hotel. They moved in a crouch, the stance of men on alert for attack. They could, if necessary, walk this way for the rest of their lives. Sometimes in 'Nam they had thought they would.

That crouch—the particular strain it caused in a man's thighs almost the instant it was assumed—always brought back the memories. Of endless patrols. Of the constant threat of death. Of the potential for attack hidden behind every bush. Of explosions beneath the feet. Or sniper bullets out of the trees.

Their eyes were trained for this. Still they hurt sometimes from the strain of so much unceasing observation. The muscles of their necks tightened. Their bodies began to stiffen in a hundred obscure joints. But like the long-distance runner who has forced his lungs to deny the excruciating pain, so they refused their bodies permission to register the ever-increasing pressures. Their knees weren't meant to take the weight this unnatural posture forced upon them. But Rosie and Cowboy could do it for a long time, past pain and the recognition of the pain. It was what Beeker had trained them to do.

Every once in a while Cowboy pointed out some feature of the landscape. "Water trap for the golf course, not deep enough to shit in." "Sand trap, great cover in a fire fight." "The beach is half a kilometer that way." Rosie didn't even nod in acknowledgment.

They didn't have to say what they both were thinking. They wanted one of the bastards real bad. Because he might lead them to Tsali. They wanted to get the kid back to Beeker before Beeker exploded. Cowboy particularly was anxious, because Cowboy felt responsible. It was his fault the kid was captured, was lost, was being tortured, was already dead. Because Cowboy should have realized that Tsali would go and do something foolish— something as foolish as what any of the Black Berets themselves might have done. That's one more reason there was a team. Leave them alone and any one of them would turn into an unrestrained Applebaum, head off gung-ho and run right at the bastards. You got a team, you got to worry about somebody else. You can't get yourself offed, 'cause your buddy might be left defenseless.

Cowboy should have kept Tsali at his side, taught the kid teamwork, taught him that he could be as important and as vital as any of the Black Berets. But now the kid was off on his own and Cowboy had to save him. Had to.

Rosie, if he had thought anything consciously at this time, would have known that he was losing it. It was going. He never understood what *it* was, really. But he sometimes knew that it was leaving him. That little, vague line that marked the boundary between civilized man and savage warrior. He was moving over into the place that had more to do with his African ancestors than the guys who wrote training manuals for the U.S. Army would ever understand.

It was a violent, steep slope he was slipping down now. Hardly ever did Rosie notice the incline till he was past stopping the descent. It was a kind of controlled insanity. Or insane control. It was even worse for Rosie than it was for Applebaum. Applebaum was forever on the brink of it, always threatening to go over, always *wanting* to go over. Rosie stepped farther back, in his good moments. But in his bad moments, he pitched forward with an eagerness and an energy that left Applebaum in the distance.

It made Rosie want to taste blood. Not just shed it. Not just see it puddled on the ground. Not just feel it splattered on his arms and neck and face. But *taste the motherfucker!* He wanted it to drip off his chin, spill down his throat, he wanted it to flow into his cupped palms so he could pour it over his shaved head and rub it into his gleaming black scalp.

There was a movement. Rosie clung to this side of sanity. *Hold it. We want a captive.* He grinned, thinking of it. A captive. What he could do to a captive. A captive reluctant to give information. Rosie liked reluctance. Rosie could have tortured pity out of Satan.

Rosie tapped Cowboy's elbow. It wasn't necessary. The flyer had already heard. He nodded. The unseen man was to their left, in the dense line of planted growth that separated the fairways of the golf course. Flush him out and he'd be in the open. They moved toward him. They each had .38 revolvers from the New Neuzen police. Great for close range, great for target practice, not so hot for anything else. But after the endless training they'd suffered at Beeker's direction, those .38's were more potent in their fists than a rifle would have been for almost anyone else.

They moved closer. Something came back to them—a lesson from 'Nam. Rosie was over six feet, Cowboy was five-ten. One of the Americans' stupidest misconceptions about the Asian enemy was that he was their same size. But the little Charlies had been much smaller. These guys were Asians, too, Indonesians, right?

So they were probably just as tiny as Charlie had been. You had to learn to look *down* to see Charlie. Way down. Never straight ahead. Both Cowboy and Rosie had heard stories of whole patrols of green grunts walking straight into ambushes that had hardly any cover to them, just 'cause they never looked *down*.

Rosie put a finger to Cowboy's wrist, and then to his own lip, signaling the flyer to shut up, be cool, let Rosie do it. The black man had figured something out. They had stealthily moved around the golf course, and were now on the northernmost edge of it. In their fatigues and all cammied up with grease, they had come to this position the long way round. The fucker hiding in the bushes was probably a spy on the hotel, or a sniper waiting for any tourists foolish enough to play a few rounds after what had happened the previous morning, on the eleventh green. He wouldn't be watching behind him, because behind him there was only dense tropical forest.

It was a risk. But Rosie was willing to go for it. After all, if the guy had been there all along and seen them, they'd be dead by now. And they weren't.

Rosie put down his .38. He stalked closer. He could smell something strange now. The odor reminded him—of what? Oh yeah—it reminded him of the streets of Saigon. This was an Asian all right—the stink of his food slopped right out of his pores, overcoming even a breeze right off a hundred thousand square miles of pure Caribbean water. The garlic, the rice wine, all that stuff Charlie ate at home—Rosie could smell it. He remembered the stinking streets of Saigon—decayed meat and rotten vegetables all cooked together in vast pots of rancid grease.

But right now he was happy for it. Right now he could home in on the enemy just with his nose. He gently pushed aside one big branch and hit paydirt so quickly he almost jumped. But the fool had made a mistake that the Black Berets never made. He thought he was just a scout, just a watcher, just a lazy sniper waiting for prey to come to him. He wasn't a real warrior, because a real warrior's always on guard, always ready, always looking for the foe who was going to creep up from behind. But not this gook . . .

Gook? thought Rosie. *What the hell do you call an Indonesian?*

With a silent tightening of his legs and a sudden spring, Rosie cleared the short distance between himself and the Indonesian. The man had heard something, for he was turning his head. But Rosie caught him there, in the side of his face, with his big black palm. A real black palm.

Rosie pressed the man's face into the hot earth of New Neuzen. The black man dropped with both knees on the man's belly, knocking all the wind out of him.

"Got him, Cowboy," Rosie said.

Still on the side of sanity.

For now.

20

Harry wandered through the eerie landscape that had once been a pine forest in Louisiana. It was still black night above, but here below, little crackling fires burned along the ground, and a few upright, denuded pines smoldered sullenly, faintly outlined in embers. These acres of Beeker's farm looked like parts of Vietnam after the B-52's had finished unloading their babies, their children of destruction, the thousand-pound bombs that left craters and barren dirt where once there had been lush jungle.

Smoke and sand lingered in the air. These unnatural clouds only added to the general impression of unreality. Harry saw there were few bodies. At least, he saw very few whole bodies. There would be a sudden arm, grotesque in its detached anatomical perfection, the cloth on the limb not even scorched. Or he would stumble on a skull, burnt and blackened, and kick it out of his path as though it were a child's ball, left in a garden path. But he wasn't looking for whole bodies anyhow. He wasn't trying to discover who the invaders had been—the tattooed triangle on all the right hands told him that—Harry just wanted to make sure none of the Black Palm assassins had survived.

Applebaum was insulted.

"What the hell are you talking about, Harry? A *survivor*? *I* set those charges, Harry. If there's a survivor, it's not my fault, it's that bitch's fault, 'cause she didn't pull the switches right. 'Cept it looked like she did, so there's not gonna be any survivors. Lay you odds, Harry."

But Harry didn't want odds. Harry needed certainty, and that's why he was checking so thoroughly. Marty was right— usually. It was very seldom that anyone got out from under one of his demolition tricks. But in this case—in every case— if just one man survived, one man still able to carry a rifle and pull a trigger, then they could be in trouble. Every seasoned professional knew that. If Harry had gotten nothing else out of Vietnam, he had got that. Seasoning.

With a growing sense of injury, Applebaum traced his friend's footsteps, pointing at all the dismembered limbs, and crying out, "Watch out, Harry, that guy's still holding a pistol and it's pointed right at us." But Harry had already seen it, and knew there was no arm attached to the hand that still held the gun. But Marty's sense that he was being insulted didn't deter Harry. The Greek plodded methodically along through the clouds of dust and smoke, stamping out ground embers as he went.

Finally Harry stood erect, his new stance a physical acknowledgment of his satisfaction. Applebaum sighed with relief. "Come on, Harry. Let's go back to the house. Tomorrow we'll get out the plow and start working this acreage over. Plow those fuckers under for fertilizer. Nothing like blood and bones to make the rice grow green. That's what Charlie used to say. Remember Charlie? Wish Charlie could have been here tonight. Guys from Indonesia, you call 'em Charlie? Maybe you call 'em Henry instead of Charlie. Hi, Henry, you old son of a gun," Marty said, waving in friendly salutation to one of the

Indonesians who looked to be buried head and shoulders in the earth. Except he wasn't buried at all. But all the other parts of him were somewhere else.

They walked back toward the house, Marty gabbling, his M-16 held loosely in his arms. Harry cradled his own as if it were a baby. He loved his rifle, not the way Marty did, but in his own way, he loved it. It smelled of spent powder; the cleaning solvents burned off when the two of them pulled their flanking movement. As soon as they had confirmed that the invading force had been armed and was up to no good, Marty and Harry had forced them into the small area where the unseen charges had been waiting to deliver their almost instantaneous death.

The lady had done it. Harry had been a little concerned, what with her fine talk and her big words about pacifism, but she had come through and had flipped the switches that saved their lives—and her own. Maybe he shouldn't have entrusted so much to her. He was a little surprised he had. But he had had faith in her, after all. That must have been it—a simple question of faith.

Then Harry began to follow Marty back toward the house. It stood on the horizon, outlined in black against the starred sky, a few hundred yards away. There, on the front porch, was the dim figure of the prime minister, distinguished by the light color of her dress. She sat there silent, unmoving. Still trying to deal with having pulled the switches, Harry thought. He wondered what it had been like for her. Had it been like the first time Harry killed in combat? When he saw the first dead body he had created himself? "Here's my friend Death, shake hands, fella." Did she want to puke the way Harry did after his first kill?

And do all those who are put to the test eventually react the way he and the other Black Berets had? Coming to accept death as an integral part of life? Arriving at the place where the killing of another human being was something that could be easily accomplished—if it had to be?

Not for the first time, Harry was thankful he was in the Black Berets, that he had Beeker to follow. What if people like him and Rosie and Marty weren't part of a team? Didn't have someone to trust? Would they just become mad, tattooed criminals like these idiots whose bodily remains littered a stretch of smoldering ground in northwestern Louisiana? Were he and Marty and Rosie and Cowboy really any different from the Indonesians?

Harry stopped short. "Jesus."

"What?" Picking up on the anxiety in Harry's voice, Marty was alert and whispering. "What is it?" His eyes scanned the farmland ahead of them, searching out what Harry had seen. As well-trained as the Greek, Marty found the target quickly enough. And just like Harry's, Marty's brain turned into a computer. It registered distance, focus, speed, darkness, all the variables. The result wasn't very good.

Two shadows, moving across the edge of the field toward the house. The two men must have been detached from the main force. They hadn't been on the computer screen, Harry didn't think. Maybe they were a rear guard. Maybe they had been late—and lucky. But whatever they were, and however they got there, they had pulled a good one. They were holding rifles, and they were getting closer to their target—the woman who sat unmoving and silent, a gray blur on the dark front porch of Beeker's house. A perfect target.

"Like our lives depended on it," said Harry slowly as he dropped to the ground. Directly beside him, Marty followed suit. At that moment Harry would have killed for a telescopic lens. Marty had his face squinted up in the sight of the M-16. "You take the one on the left," said Harry.

Marty agreed. The two Black Berets wrapped their rifles' slings around their left arms, made their elbows as stiff as possible. The slightest movement of the rifles would ruin their aim at this distance. Harry's M-16 was on automatic—he assumed Marty's was too. At least they'd have a chance for follow-up shots. That was in their favor. They'd need it—the two surviving Black Palm assassins were dressed in black, moving through blackness. Only now and then did some glimmer of skin or metal betray their precise position.

There was no use in trying to warn the woman. Any sound they made would only alert the attackers as well. Nor was there any cause to try to move closer. The attackers might pause at any moment, take aim, and kill Beatrix VanderVolt.

"Now." Harry spoke the word easily. He almost always spoke calmly. But the spurting of his M-16 wasn't calm. It was loud and it was deadly. The first of the thirty rounds of ammunition dug up dirt a foot from the shadowy right-hand target. The man—not a Black Beret who would have taken life-preserving advantage of the warning—froze rather than diving for cover. The line of bullets moved at astonishing speed. A couple more spat up earth, but then Harry had corrected his aim. The legs of the man seemed to explode as a dozen bullets ripped through cloth, flesh, and bone. Harry, who had done this before, didn't correct his aim further. He let the man collapse into the metal storm, let the man's belly drop down to meet the river of steel, let the man's head slip uncontrollably and directly into the line of fire. It snapped back and burst.

Only then did Harry turn and look at Marty's target. He, too, was laid out on the ground. Undoubtedly dead.

"You wasted a lot of ammunition, Harry. Lot of waste there," said Marty, shaking his head. "I got mine with one shot. Just one shot. I'm as bad as Beeker with this thing now. Bad as Beeker!"

Harry—as always—ignored Marty's crowing and moved cautiously toward the corpses. To his consternation, he found a single bullet hole through the back of the head of Marty's target. "You crazy son of a bitch," the Greek said, "why'd you stop? Why did you take that chance? You should have sent more lead in there."

"I am as bad as the Beak, Greek, I don't need no second tries. Look, didn't even put mine on automatic, 'cause I knew . . . I *knew* . . ."

Harry just sighed.

21

Rosie was smiling. The little man whose skin was still encrusted with the dirt from the golf course couldn't duplicate the black man's grin. The Indonesian captive was back down on one of the luxurious beds of the Carib Beach Hotel, fourth floor, with a view overlooking the sea. The little man hadn't ever seen the inside of a place like this, except as a houseboy maybe. But here he was, baby naked, and his hands and feet stretched and corded to the bed. Rosie was alone in the room with him, watching, waiting.

The door opened and Beeker walked in with one of the New Neuzen constables. The newcomer, Corporal Achin, was one of the polyglot remainders of the once farflung Dutch empire. All the races flowed in his veins, but his East Indian heritage was dominant. Their common ancestry made Achin hate this terrorist all the more.

Achin had spent his whole life becoming a New Neuzener. He and his parents and his brothers and sisters had tried to integrate themselves into the new race that was ruling in this tiny tropical paradise. He had fought other kids when they had taunted him about his background and told him to go back to Java. "This is my homeland!" he had cried in anger. He had proved himself loyal over and over again. He had observed the rituals of the republic with more fervor than anyone else. He had never put on his uniform but with a sense of pride in his adopted country.

This piece of meat tied to the bed, who called himself a man, was the embodiment of betrayal to Achin, the one whose presence and actions on New Neuzen would be a stigma for Achin and his children for decades. All their work at becoming full members of Prime Minister VanderVolt's visionary new society would be erased by the stupid and careless, blind and immature posturings of this fool and his comrades.

"*Kill him!*" Achin demanded in English. "Kill him now!" His small fists were clenched, his voice was a straining bellows of hatred. Beeker stood between the police officer and the captive.

"We got to get some information from him first. We got to find my son. They have him, and I want him back. We need you to translate."

"I want to see him die."

"You will," said Rosie. "You'll have lots of time to watch him die. Lots. But first he talks."

There was something in Rosie's face that calmed Achin, made him slow down. Achin stared for a few moments in Rosie's eyes. Maybe the black man knew what the New Neuzen policeman felt, maybe Rosie had suffered for every stupid act that a black idiot had committed in America, his own country. Take one step forward and some fool drags you ten steps back. *Yes*, Achin thought, *this man knows*.

Beeker sensed an agreement between the two of them. He continued, "Van Waring says this one's pidgin's not too good. In pain, he might start speaking his own language. That's why we need you."

Panic had creased the captive Indonesian's eyes during this

exchange in English. He knew it concerned him, and boded him no good. He opened his eyes when Achin tossed a set of Asian words at him, but his eyes remained blank. Achin tried another set of words. The captive still said nothing, but in his eyes appeared the unmistakable light of angered comprehension.

"I told him his mother's cunt stinks like monkey shit," explained Achin. "He understood that. He speaks Javanese. I can translate. Get him to talk."

"Give the guy a chance," said Beeker. "Just ask him where the headquarters is, where they'd keep the boy."

Achin shot a stream of Javanese at the captive. Rosie smiled when he saw the naked man's jaw jut out in defiance.

Rosie walked toward the bed, grinning. He looked up just a little and saw the same look on Achin's face: The New Neuzen policeman didn't want to miss out either. *And if this fool thinks we like it,* Rosie mused, *so much the better.*

Rosie started easy. Just the usual. Just the things that let a man know it's gonna hurt and it's gonna hurt like hell and it's never gonna stop. Rosie had a knife in his hand. One he had picked out purposefully. It was the dullest knife he could find in the kitchen. Sharp knives are too clean, too easy. They cut through flesh so quickly that there's no sensation to the injury. But dull ones, they're great! They work.

Dull knives sawed through flesh. They tore the skin, they dragged at the meat, they pulled at the muscles. Dull knives hurt.

Rosie just picked up one of the guy's tiny nipples and held it between his thumb and forefinger. Then he began to saw underneath with the knife. The man began instantly to scream. That was just fear, Rosie knew. The pain would come a few seconds later. The screams changed pitch suddenly—lower. *That* was the pain. Beeker looked on stoically; he'd seen it all before, and his only thought now was to find his son.

Rosie sawed the nipple free from the captive's chest, leaving a raw bleeding hole there. The man's screams weren't real yet. Just the usual clean screams a man gives out merely from physical pain. They weren't the *I'm going to die* screams, or the *Please let me die* screams. "You can try him," said Rosie, "but I don't think he's ready yet."

Achin spit out more words. The man's eyes were filled with tears, but the jaw came back out, resolute as before.

"Okay, pal," said Rosie cheerfully, and went to work on the other nipple.

Beeker had not even shut the hotel room door. The man's screams echoed down the deserted corridor. All the tourists had left earlier in the day. If anyone in the hotel objected to a little torture on the fourth floor, he didn't present himself to complain about it.

Soon Rosie had two little pieces of dark flesh between his fingers.

The man screamed once more—a scream of protest rather than pain.

Beeker spoke up from the corner, "Do this fast. No one deserves this shit."

"Hold his head up," said Rosie to Achin. "I want him to see what I'm gonna do next." The New Neuzen policeman put his hand under the terrorist's head, and propped it up.

With a kind of surgical precision, marred only by the blunt edge of the blade, Rosie pricked the man's skin right at his neck. Then he tore the flesh with the knife point down the chest, across the stomach, over the abdomen and right to the base of the captive's shriveled cock. Blood oozed up and formed a perfectly straight blue-red line, neatly dividing the man's torso.

Rosie followed the line back up with the flat of the knife, turning his wrist one way and then the other, flaying the flesh back and showing the horrified captive the red and purple interior of his body. He stuck one big black finger inside, and wiggled it. "Feel that?" he asked. "That's your liver."

Achin smilingly translated.

The captive writhed—the sensation of being prodded *inside* his body was new, and terrible.

"Try again," suggested Beeker.

Achin spoke. The defiance was gone from the terrorist's eyes and jaw. His tears had dried up. He looked up at the black torturer and saw something there he had never seen before—at least not to such a degree. A kind of complacent, casual, offhand cruelty.

"That's right," said Rosie soothingly, for he had interpreted the look correctly, "there's more, and it gets worse. So talk, or you'll find out what's down the line."

Achin translated. The man wanted to talk, but fear stopped his throat.

A low moan came from the captive, a moan that Beeker knew. It was the sound a man makes when he knows he's going to die. When his only hope is to die quickly. When he'll trade anything he has for that privilege of speed. "He'll talk now," said Beeker.

Achin barked again. The captive's words came slowly. The tone was even, faltering, resigned. It was the way a man talks when he's being honest, because honesty is all he has strength left for.

Achin translated: "There's a cave under the cliffs on the northwest side of the island. You can only get in underwater at high tide, but at low tide there's an entrance. That's where they're headquartered."

"And the boy . . ." said Beeker grimly.

Achin spoke a few words, and the captive responded without further prompting. A few moments later Achin translated: "They brought a boy in. But this man doesn't know if he's still alive or not. They might keep him for ransom, if they think his parents are rich. Or they might just get rid of him. Or they might . . ."

Achin paused.

"*Might what?*" Beeker demanded.

Achin glanced away. "Use the boy," he said quietly. "Sexually."

The captive was speaking again. He spoke in Javanese but his words didn't need translating. *I've told you what you want. Now let me go.*

Beeker reached down to the place where the captive's chest had been split open. His hands pushed the skin apart. The Cherokee's eyes glazed with primal anger as he stared in the Black Palm's face. Then—watching the man's face contort with fear and pain such as he'd never felt—Beeker found the beating heart. He took the pumping organ in his right hand and squeezed, digging his fingers into pulsing muscle, choking off the movement. The man screamed, flailed against his bonds, and died when Beeker burst his heart open in his bare hand.

22

In the light of dawn, Harry and Marty made yet another search of the area. The computer security system hadn't picked up any movement, but Harry was concerned that Marty's explosions might have thrown off some of the sensors. When he returned from New Neuzen, Cowboy would have to check the whole thing out before Harry would fully trust it again.

The two men were dead tired, not having dared sleep during the night for fear that yet another survivor might come after the prime minister—and them. They stood guard, Marty hidden in the large bushes at the front of the house, Harry in the control room.

Harry had spoken to Beatrix VanderVolt briefly, to make sure she was all right. Pulling the switches had been difficult for her, as Harry surmised. Her view of the world and her place in that world had changed irrevocably. But she was a strong woman, and even though the danger was past, she still didn't break down. At least not in front of him.

But Harry saw sadness in her eyes to match his own.

By noon Marty and Harry were convinced that their victory had been absolute. They even found the two vans the assailants had used for transport. The vehicles had been rented, so Harry called the airport and told the agency where they could be found, making up a story about a "change in plans."

Exhausted, he took a shower and then, dressed in clean clothes, stepped out onto the porch with a cold can of Budweiser in his hand. How many times, he wondered, had he tried to wash away the acrid taste of death with a bottle of beer . . .

"What the hell are you doing?" he demanded of the prime minister of New Neuzen.

Beatrix VanderVolt, the hope of the Third World, was seated on the edge of the porch, her legs spread wide apart on the steps, plucking the feathers from a dead chicken.

"Starting dinner," she replied matter-of-factly. "You two must be starved by now, and I'm going to fix you the best pot of gumbo you ever tasted."

Harry just stared, and then realized that Mrs. VanderVolt must also have wrung the chicken's neck herself. He hadn't done it, and Marty was sleeping on the living room couch. There was something quite primitive about her posture, about her activity, and about whatever had driven her to do this. Something sad about it, sad and ancient. The woman preparing a meal for the husband and son returning from battle.

That's what pulling those switches had done to Beatrix VanderVolt. It had brought out the most primitive archetype of woman in her. Harry doubted if anyone in the world had seen her like this. He had seen a photograph of her in yesterday's paper, in an evening gown, dancing with the President.

Harry glanced away from her. In some ways he'd like to be able to look away from all women. He stared straight ahead, at the series of craters where yesterday there had been a three-acre stand of stunted pine. The sun high overhead cast defining shadows only at the very edges of the wide, overlapping holes in the ground. He was reminded of Vietnam. And just the sight of those holes Applebaum's bombs had made forced him to see something else from Vietnam that he was always trying to forget—but never had. The thing that had brought sadness into his eyes to stay.

Her name had been Mei. In her own language he called her the Flower of the Orient. That overstatement was an indication of how badly he'd fallen for her. He fell hard. So hard, he married her.

The military ceremony was complete with crossed swords and dress uniforms. He was happy, for the first time in his life. Fully happy. Now he realized that those few months he was married to Mei would be the only time in his entire life when he knew what that feeling was.

They had an apartment in Hue, the Imperial City, the ancient home of the Vietnamese emperors, a city of canals and flowers, perfumes and painted beauty in the midst of a country tearing itself apart in war and death. He must have performed his military duties each day, though now he remembered only the off-hours he spent with Mei. They must have eaten meals together, must have walked the streets with one another, but he remembered none of that. He only remembered when they were in bed. And Harry maintained years, decades, of memories of time spent in passionate embrace with Mei.

His life—for once—seemed to make sense. He had little notion of what happened outside of Hue, outside his house, outside his bedroom, outside the narrow bed they shared. He listened as his friends talked of battles and the dead, and they might have been talking of Napoleon's losses or victories in Russia. The American war in Asia was a distracting sideshow to the real business of his life—Mei.

Then a friend—was it a friend?—from Counterintelligence told Harry about the story that ended his happiness. Over a beer they shared early one hot afternoon, this "friend" told Harry about a roundup of Vietcong spies the ARVN was planning. This "friend" knew about it because he was liaison between U.S. forces and the South Vietnamese army. It was going to be a knockout blow to the communist plan to infiltrate and take over Hue.

The ARVN had learned about the whole network almost by chance. A piece of data here, a confession there, a lucky discovery afterward. The pieces that never seemed to come together for the ARVN did this time. They had the whole goddamned Charlie conspiracy down to the last eight-year-old informer.

The "friend" went on. He said—

Harry closed his eyes and wished himself out of Vietnam, out of that hot little cafe in Hue, and back onto the front porch in Louisiana, with the prime minister of New Neuzen plucking a chicken on the steps below him. But once the story started running in his mind, it played out to the end. Harry couldn't stop it. He was back in Hue.

The "friend" told Harry that the head of the infiltrating network was a beautiful Vietnamese woman who had just married a SEAL. She was hiding behind her new husband, using his household—paid for with U.S. government funds— as headquarters for the underground movement. No one would ever have suspected her. But now they knew. And that very night the ARVN was going to get her, take her in, and torture her for every scrap of VC information she held in her subtle, traitorous brain. The "friend" didn't have to tell Harry the woman's name.

It was Mei.

They made love one last time. Only she didn't know it was the last time. It seemed impossible that Harry's fervor could be so much greater than it had ever been before—but that was the case. One last time. With every thrust he prayed she would kill him.

When they were done, that last time, she went into the bathroom. As always she ran a tub of hot water for them to bathe in together. Harry followed her in, naked, carrying his service revolver.

Before he killed her there was one thing he wanted to know. One thing he had to know. But he didn't ask.

She knelt naked at the side of the tub, her hand dissolving the pellets of soft, scented soap in the water. To kill her now was a favor to her. Her death at his hand would be quick, sudden, surprising, painless. Her death at the hands of the ARVN would be none of those things. To be forced to kill the one thing in the world that had made him happy was Harry's own punishment for allowing himself to be betrayed.

One thing he had to know.

But before he asked, he brought up the pistol and fired. Just once, as she was turning her head to welcome him.

Her head burst open, and the gray stuff of her brain splattered on the white porcelain. Her long shiny black hair waved in the air like weeds beneath slowly flowing water. Her body slumped forward. Her blood swirled pink in the warm, scented water.

Harry never found out the answer to the question he did not ask.

Had she loved him? Had their marriage been true despite her identity, despite her betrayal of his country, despite her plotting and her duplicity and her lies?

Or had her marriage to him been a plot, carefully conceived, flawlessly executed, maintained with a passion that was as false as it had been intense?

The remainder of Harry's life would be spent flinging himself back and forth between the two possibilities, now on the one side, now on the other, believing Mei false in one moment, as false as Jezebel. Believing her true in the next, as true as the most faithful wife who had ever spoken vows of marriage, trust, and fidelity. And he could never convince himself that the answer didn't matter, that had he asked he would still have killed her, no matter what reply Mei gave him.

The story played out. The last image, as always, her blood swirling pink in the warm, scented water. Harry looked down at Beatrix VanderVolt. He hadn't wanted a woman in a long time. He realized with a start that he wanted this one. Despite Mei. Despite the unanswered question. Or because of it. Or because the sadness in the prime minister's eyes matched his own. Because she had killed when her whole life was a fight against murder and war. Because Beatrix VanderVolt now could understand a little of what Harry was, and what Harry suffered. She was a handsome woman, only forty or so, not much older than he was. Deep chocolate skin. Full breasts. Her body full and mature, but still sleek with lines of activity. Sensuous mouth. He had seen her looking at him. He had . . .

He didn't think about it anymore.

He bent over and swooped her up in his enormous, hairy arms.

She squeaked—the way a teen-age girl squeaks. But then her arms went around his neck. The faces were a foot apart. Their eyes locked in a cool, detached, almost despairing passion.

She did understand. Harry knew it.

He leaned his head forward and pressed his unopened lips against the side of her mouth. That was all that was necessary. Still carrying her in his arms, he turned and went into the house.

In the humid noonday heat the slam of the screen door behind them was dull and muffled. You had heat like that in Hue.

23

Clad only in the swimming briefs he'd been wearing when he slipped on the weed-encrusted rocks, Tsali was bound hand and foot with rope. Behind him the two knots were joined by a third length, which was wound around a small upright pillar of waterbeaten stone inside the cave occupied by the Black Palm. He'd been standing upright all the rest of that day and through the night, sleeping only fitfully. Over and over he counted the men occupying the cavern, always with the result of between fifty-one and fifty-five. Because of their movement and because of the deep shadows and fitful lighting of the cavern, it was not possible for him to be more accurate than that.

Since he'd been there, the tide had risen—drowning the low entrance. No one had come or departed during the hours of high tide. Low tide had come late in the night, and a small party of the Indonesians had departed in a black inflatable raft. They'd carried weapons with them, Russian AK-47's. The men in the cave might have been surprised to know that the sixteen-year-old American boy they'd found on the rocks could have handled that complex bit of machinery every bit as well as the best of them. Of course, not everybody had Marty Applebaum as an instructor.

It was morning now. The tide was coming in again, but still bright daylight could be seen through the entrance to the space. Tsali's eyes were so accustomed to the darkness of the cavern, and the small illumination provided by oil lamps, that the sunlight seemed painfully bright as it glanced off the clear surface of the cove.

The men in the group had all risen, complainingly. And now they were having a pep rally. Tsali didn't have to understand the language to know that that was what was happening. Exhortation from the leader, cheering from the crowd. Promise from the leader, more cheering from the crowd. Cajoling from the leader, riotous cheering from the crowd.

They were getting ready to go out. The black inflatable rafts were tethered to stakes driven between crevices in the rocks. They bumped lazily against one another in the dark water. The AK-47's were laid out haphazardly and there were two piles of satchel charges off to one side. Not with precision and neatness the way the Black Berets would have set out their weapons, but with unconcern and shrugging laziness.

Tied as he was, Tsali felt only contempt, but he knew that even the lazy or careless can kill.

The leader, a man no more than Tsali's size but still bigger than all the rest, reached the climax of his oration, and the cheering went on and on and on. It echoed in the chamber, filling Tsali's head. The men grabbed the weapons, got into the boats, and paddled out toward the light-filled hole in the far wall of the cavern. Soon all five black rafts had sailed through with the three dozen men aboard them, and the last of their cheers died away.

Tsali looked around the cavern. Nine men leaving the night before. Thirty-six going now. Six still remaining. Fifty-one altogether.

He studied the six men remaining. If they were men. He hadn't been sure at first. When he'd been roused to consciousness in the night, he'd taken them for women as they moved about in the light of the oil lamps, dressed in long sheaths of brightly patterned cloth wrapped securely round their slender bodies. They'd prepared food, passed it around, cleaned up afterward, all the while chattering in shrill voices. And Tsali had heard their cries in the black night, mimicked cries of female passion, parodies of what he'd heard from Ruth and Jocelyn. The Black Palm had not brought any women with them to New Neuzen, but they had brought the next best thing. Punks. Prison whores. Men who would act as women.

Now only they were left. Even among themselves, with the fighting men gone, they giggled and pranced and acted as women. Tsali watched and said nothing, made no motion. He had been put out of the way. He had been poked and prodded the night before, and the fact of his muteness had been got across. Perhaps it was that that had saved him. He didn't know. Perhaps the Black Palm intended on ransoming him. He wasn't sure. But Tsali did feel that his continued safety depended on his appearing as weak and as inconspicuous as possible.

An hour after the men had left, the "women" all sat down on the rocks with bottles of beer and began to play dominoes by the light of an oil lamp. After a while this broke into squabbling, and one of the women dashed the game pieces into the water, and the game was broken up. After the little altercation dissipated into more giggling, these she-males looked about for something to occupy them, and their eyes finally alighted on Tsali. They pointed, they laughed, they waded through the water that separated the rock on which Tsali was held captive from the much larger space where they handled the cooking for the group. They raised their dresses high, and made little clucking noises as they crossed.

Like degenerate mermaids tormenting a stranded sailor, they reached up to him out of the water, and poked at him obscenely, and made sly comments, and rolled their eyes, and laughed. They gabbled about him in their language, but one of them spoke English, for out of the gabble, Tsali heard the words, "Little Man, Little Man . . ."

This one climbed up on the rock right at Tsali's feet. S/he spoke to him in heavily accented English. "So, Little Man, today is the day. Today is the birthday of Kota Jutan, the new republic of the oppressed peoples of Indonesia. Our husbands will raise today the flag of Kota Jutan and I will be the new First Lady . . ." Here the she-male turned to his/her friends, and spoke several sentences in a high, wheedling voice that sent them all in gales of shrill laughter. Then s/he turned back to Tsali and said, in a sultry, insinuating voice, "And when our husbands return in victory we will give them a new present. No more Little Man. We will call you Liam . . ."

All the she-males giggled.

"Liam means Little Wife," explained the one who spoke English. S/he slid off the rock back into the water. They all waded back toward the kitchen area of the cavern. "We will prepare a gown for you . . ." s/he called back with a flirtatious wave of the head.

Tsali spit contemptuously into the rising water.

24

Tsali had worked hard to free himself, constantly rubbing the ropes that bound his wrists against the rock to which he had been bound. But he discovered that this trick works better in movies and on television than it does in real life. The rope was thick and new. The rock was smooth and slippery. His arms grew tired and stiff.

An hour passed. The water was at full high tide, and the entrance to the cave was submerged. In that direction only a small area of glowing blue water, shimmering with the refracted sunlight outside, showed where the water gained entrance to the cavern. The air grew stuffy inside, and it was dark. He could see the "women" in their area. They were eating, laughing, and calling out to him now and again. "Liam! Liam!"

Because the light from the outside was almost entirely cut off, the cavern was dark. He could see the she-males, because of the lighted lamps they kept near them. He was confident that they could not see him, or that at best, he was but a dim shadow in a dark corner.

Tsali watched them as they prepared for him a sheathlike gown very much like the ones they themselves wore. The one who spoke English, and appeared to be the leader of this perverse group, waded across the small inlet of water that separated their area from the rock on which Tsali stood. A second followed, holding a lamp. The others remained behind, but they stood at the edge of the water, and pointed, and giggled, and called out to him in their unnaturally shrill voices.

Tsali felt very strange. He had been standing up for more than twenty-four hours, bound all that time, with nothing to eat. He was weary, and worried—not about himself, but about Cowboy, and about his father. He was in a lightless cavern, cut off from the rest of the world. And wading through the shallow water toward him was this oddly formal and stately procession of two men dressed as women, their faces made up as women, their movements a parody of women's walks and women's gestures. One holding aloft a lamp, the other carrying a gown on his/her outstretched arms.

"My name is Tiang," said the one who spoke English as s/he approached the rock to which Tsali was bound. "I am to be your mother, Liam. I have brought a gown for your wedding. I will bathe you. I will prepare your body for the wedding night. My daughter Liam will be greatly desired by the warriors returning from battle. My daughter's wedding night will be without end, as her mother Tiang's was."

There were no more taunts from the women. They were silent, solemn.

Tsali slumped back against the rock, and would have slipped to his knees had not the ropes held him in place. His eyes half closed themselves in weariness.

Tiang placed the gown on the rock at Tsali's feet. Then, with an odd sort of grace, s/he clambered up beside the Cherokee boy. The lamp-bearer came closer and spoke some words in a low gabbling voice to Tiang.

Tiang shook his/her head no in reply, and held out a hand. The lamp-bearer, evidently with some reluctance, took a knife from a fold in his/her own gown, and handed it to Tiang.

"My daughter is weak," said Tiang. "Weak because she is hungry. Weak because she has not slept. Weak because she is afraid. But Liam's mother Tiang will protect her. And bathe her. And prepare her for her wedding night."

With that Tiang reached behind Tsali, and sawed in two the rope that bound his hands to his feet.

Tsali collapsed on the rock, his hands still tied behind him. He would have slid into the water had not Tiang's strong hand grabbed the elastic of his swim suit and pulled him back.

"Tiang will dress her daughter Liam," said Tiang, as she slit the ropes that bound Tsali's wrists. When she did so, the boy's hands just fell limply against the rock. Tiang raised them to his/her lips and kissed them, and then rubbed them to restore circulation. Tsali stirred and opened his mouth as if to moan—though no sound came out.

"Tiang will feed her daughter Liam," said Tiang, and sliced the ropes that bound Tsali's feet. She chafed his bruised ankles.

The "women" on the rock opposite were singing, softly, a strange melody that echoed in the dark cavern.

Tiang stood behind Tsali and caught his limp body tenderly beneath his/her arms. "Rise, my daughter Liam," Tiang said, as s/he lifted the boy up.

In one forceful motion, Tsali kicked directly out and caught the hand of the lamp-bearer. She screamed and the lamp pitched forward in the water and was immediately extinguished.

With his elbows lashing backward, Tsali caught Tiang in the shoulder and chest. S/he staggered back a step in the darkness.

Tsali dived into the water.

It was frigidly cold, and so shallow that his chest scraped

along rocks and sand on the bottom. But he swam underwater, toward that glimmering blue light that marked the entrance of the cave. He'd had time for but one short breath, and he rose to the surface to take another.

As he did so, the cave was suddenly filled with the overpowering noise and reverberating echo of gunfire. One of the women was man enough to employ an AK-47 at least. The bullets spit into the water at Tsali's left. He dived again, went as deep as he could, and swam toward the light.

More bullets spilled into the water above him, but quickly lost their direction and speed.

The water grew lighter and clearer around him. He saw the curving walls of the entrance to the cave, swam between them, then turned toward shore and went another twenty yards before he dared surface among the rocks.

All was quiet.

Floating nearby was a piece of the wreckage from Doc Wilhelm's boat, wedged in between two half-submerged boulders.

And on the beach a solitary figure, standing as if waiting for him.

And maybe she was.

Delilah.

25

Beeker and Cowboy lay facedown in the sand trap, cradling the wonderful BARs in their arms. Ready for the enemy.

Not quite ready for the enemy. Cowboy's concentration was off. He was thinking about the kid. And thinking about Beeker thinking about the kid. And the kid—if he was still alive—thinking about Beeker. What if one of them died? What would the other do? What would Cowboy do? How to console Beeker for the loss of the one thing he'd ever really wanted, a son? How to tell Tsali that the father he'd found at last had been shot up by these idiot terrorists?

For Christ's sake, he wasn't supposed to be thinking like this. He was just supposed to be a soldier in the field, carrying a rifle, offing the enemy, doing the good John Wayne stuff where you go in, shoot off your weapon, kill the enemy who's polite enough not to stink or shit or look surprised or come back to haunt your dreams.

Why wasn't life like John Wayne movies? It'd be so much easier. Good guys and bad guys. The bad guys die. They die with neat little holes in their bodies, and the blood doesn't even soak their clothes. Then before the bodies start to stink in the sun and turn black and get covered with flies and beetles, the good guy smiles and grabs a broad by the ass and heads off for that bar where the bartender never charges a good guy, no matter how much he drinks. John Wayne doesn't worry about guilt and responsibility. John Wayne doesn't have to worry that sometimes the bad guys fire back, and sometimes a bullet catches the good guy in the neck, and he dies with a long red gurgle and a load of shit in his britches. *If the movies got this stuff right, maybe we wouldn't have to do this so often.*

Cowboy smelled his sweat. He could smell a stink coming from Beeker too. They were nervous. They should be nervous. They were going to fight soon and the only thing they knew was going to happen was that people were going to die. A man who had lived thirty-six years and three months and seventeen days was going to go to hell this afternoon, instead of waiting around to increase that last number to eighteen. Fate was going to freeze him at 36-3-17. And that was going to happen to a whole bunch of guys. And it might even happen to Cowboy. Get his statistics frozen.

So they had blown up the bridge on the road that led from New Neuzen's northwest coast down to New Delft. Bad job of it too. The New Neuzen ammunitions expert was all right, for somebody who probably hadn't had a lot of experience destroying infrastructure lately, but Cowboy couldn't help but compare his job to what Applebaum would have done. When you saw one of Marty's explosions, you got the same feeling as when you looked at a goddamn wedding cake in seven fucking tiers—*artistry.*

Anyway, with a couple of tries, the bridge was gone. And so the Black Palm, if they were coming from the north, would have to skirt around that road. And the only way to do that was to go over the golf course, and go over this little bridge here. The little bridge, painted bright red, that arched over the shallow creek that served as water trap on nine of the golf course's eighteen holes.

It was a trade-off. Blow that big bridge and you could force the Black Palm to move the way you wanted them to. Get them all over here in this narrow, open space. But you also alerted them. Let them know that somebody was preparing for them.

Cowboy wondered how many there were of the Black Palm. Delilah's reports said about ninety altogether, but maybe not all of them were planted in New Neuzen. Maybe not all of them would be coming down to New Delft today, to pick up a few souvenirs, rape a few natives, off a few tourists. Figure on fifty, Cowboy decided. And how many on the good guys' side? Fifteen. Including him and Beeker, and Rosie on the hotel roof. Not bad. Better odds than usual. Better allies than usual too. Damn, he didn't want to forget to buy that Van Waring a beer. Rosie had a new friend too. Rosie and Achin. Shared interest in torturing people to death. Yeah, Rosie says to this guy, let's go have a couple of beers and rip somebody's tongue out . . .

Cowboy grinned, a little grin just for himself. This was the sort of thing he always thought about before battle. And when the battle was going, and when it was over, he never remembered the long winding trails of thought that had coiled inside his brain as he waited for the thing to begin. Worrying about buying somebody a beer, wondering if your buddy was gonna get his statistics frozen, sniffing to see if you stink as bad as the guy next to you, making up funny little conversations and moving your lips as you spoke both parts in your mind, deciding whether to piss your pants or to try to find a safe tree . . .

The plan was simple. Let the guerrillas move across the golf course bridge unchallenged. Let them get half their forces on this side of the bridge, and then that little cop who wasn't quite as good as Applebaum could jerk his switches.

Wait for them to split their forces.

Wait for them to show up at all.

Just wait.

That was the lot of the warrior. That was always the hardest part. The bullets and the noise of the explosions would last two minutes, maybe not even that. Most everybody who was going to die would be dead by the time the echoes died out. A lingerer took maybe five minutes more. All that part was easy because you didn't have to think about it. You just did it. And in the end you were either dead, or you were still alive, thinking *I could have got my statistics frozen back there . . .*

But the hard part was before that. The waiting, the watching, the listening. They wore you down. Beeker had forced them to wait so often, just to be used to it, that Cowboy felt like some kind of fucked-up Zen Buddhist with all the waiting.

He remembered their training, when Beeker would make them crouch in a ditch by the side of the road until that one moment when there wasn't anybody within five miles to see them run across the highway in a crouch and leap into the ditch over there. Waiting, just training to wait like they were some kind of fucked-up monks on an Asian mountain.

Cowboy scowled as he turned to look at Beeker. Then the scowl and the complaint disappeared. The bastard was waiting himself, waiting to know if his son was alive.

Motors. The enemy.

The waiting became tense.

The line of vehicles was led by a Jeep. Mounted on the back of it an M-30 on a heavy metal stand. Two men flanking it, one to feed ammunition, the other to fire. Even from a distance Cowboy could see worry in the faces of the two men.

If the road bridge had been blown, this golf course bridge might be an ambush.

Behind the lead Jeep, two more, and then a couple of trucks. They were all standard military issue vehicles, but had been painted in bright colors. Two of the Jeeps had names of New Delft hotels painted on the sides. The third was simply a bright pink. One of the trucks bore the logo of an island linen service and the other was decorated with large panels depicting tropical sunsets. Real camouflage on an island devoted to tourism. The small convoy looked like a motley circus parade as it dug through the soft ground of the golf course, ripping up two dozen years of careful hotel maintenance.

Cowboy knew instantly that the Black Palm had brought in the cars and trucks over a long period of time. No suspicion had been aroused. Fuck, they looked stupid right now, ice-cream green and yellow and a pink Jeep with an M-30 mounted on its rear end—but it didn't change the fact that the vehicles contained weapons and men to fire them.

Cowboy moved to take aim. Beeker put a restraining hand on his arm and shook his head silently. *Not yet.*

Waiting, always waiting.

The Black Palm were smarter than Cowboy thought they'd be. They stopped the line of vehicles several yards from the bridge. Their chattering Asian voices came to Cowboy on a puff of wind. The driver of the lead Jeep climbed down and walked over to the bridge. He sidled down the embankment, and after a few moments yelled back in one of the Malay dialects.

"Shit," said Beeker in a whisper. Cowboy knew they'd found the bombs. Now they could disengage them, if they had someone who knew how. Another man, probably their own Martin Applebaum, ran to the front of the line and joined the other under the bridge.

"Now?" Cowboy asked.

"No. Same plan."

Just let them go through, let them cut their forces in half. Wait. Fucking wait.

The Indonesian Applebaum was pleased with himself. He climbed up out of the creek ditch and held up the severed wire to show his comrades. They cheered in their shrill, squeaking voices.

Cowboy just wanted to get it over with. Now. Just get it over with. His fingers itched on the old BAR he was holding. He wanted some powder to put on his hands.

"Shit," Beeker said again. "Holy shit."

Cowboy hadn't expected mortars. Why the hell did they think that the Indonesians would only have rifles? Why hadn't they planned properly for this Asian enemy?

The dull cylinders of metal were deceptive in appearance. Looked so innocent. Two members of the Black Palm were setting them up in a line, a dozen of the two-foot tubes. They pointed in the air at an exaggerated tilt. Aimed toward the hotel. They probably thought the tourists were still in there.

No more tourists, though.

Just Rosie and Van Waring and the fifteen most decent men on the whole goddamn island of New Neuzen. And one woman—he'd almost forgotten her. Delilah.

"We gotta stop 'em," said Cowboy. He had estimated their number. Thirty-five, forty maybe. He and Beeker could probably stop the mortars, but that would give the others time to escape, to retreat back to their fortress, back to where Tsali was being held hostage.

Cowboy knew that Beeker was thinking the same thing, and that Beeker was making a decision. He could let the Indonesians fire on the hotel, and get a better chance at killing them all. Or he could stop the mortars, and put Tsali—if Tsali were still alive—at continued, or even greater, risk.

Beeker made the decision. He lifted his BAR to his shoulder. Cowboy followed the motion. They were ready. He could have sworn he heard Billy Leaps pressing the trigger. That was impossible, but he could have sworn that he did. The two BARs spit out lead at precisely the same moment. Absolutely the same moment.

The Indonesians had been kneeling, fourteen of them. Kneeling to set up the mortars, probably intending to fire them all at once. Mostly there was one man to a weapon, but some extras had come along to give their friends a helping hand. And join their friends in death. The line of terrorists collapsed, from either end toward the middle. Twin lines of bullets dug up the earth, and dug out flesh, and spewed blood across the edge of the seventeenth green. By the time the two lines of bullets met in the middle, the Indonesians there had got to their feet and were running away. Which only meant that Cowboy and Beeker's bullets got them in the back, and they pitched forward and died with the smell of grass in their nostrils.

Even before the shooting stopped, the remaining Indonesians understood the vulnerability of their position. Gears screamed as the trucks and Jeeps were revved up and thrown into reverse.

Cowboy and Beeker's position in the sand trap was a good one. They were able to duck down and reload quickly and easily. They simply ignored the noise of the return fire from the M-30's on the Jeeps. The Black Palm had no way of knowing their strength. If the Indonesians had realized there were only two men with guns, they might have been willing to cross the bridge and continue the assault. But fourteen dead men on the grass argued for a lot of firepower, and the Indonesians remained on the far side.

Beeker and Cowboy finished reloading at the same moment.

They flipped over, and raised their BARs above the lip of the trap. Beeker fired, with the weapon on automatic. Got two. Taking aim at the driver of the lead Jeep through the windshield, Cowboy squeezed the BAR trigger.

The windshield exploded, and something behind it too.

Cowboy and Beeker stood up. The Indonesians were in retreat. One of Beeker's bullets found the gasoline tank of the yellow and green Jeep. A *whooosh* of fired gasoline engulfed the vehicle, and the three unfortunate men inside it became little black stick figures, sitting rigid and probably already dead as they burned.

It was the perfect cover. Cowboy jammed a new clip home as he jumped up over the lip of the sand trap. He ran forward, his BAR sending its bullets into the truck directly behind the burning Jeep. It was trying to back up. Cowboy got the radiator. Steam geysered up, and the truck's retreat was slowed.

Cowboy knew—he just understood—that Beeker was behind him. Their partnership was that solid, that close.

They raced across the green, the place misleadingly manicured for the pleasure of men who'd fly fifteen hundred miles for the pleasure of a game of golf, now turned suddenly into a field of deadly combat. They ran, their guns firing. They ran screaming, their lungs emptying in a primal shout of warrior glory.

Cowboy knelt, took aim at the driver of the second Jeep through the bright canvas door.

No response. The weapon was jammed.

Suddenly, Cowboy was naked. Like a newborn baby. Holding a weapon that was about as useful to him as an umbilical cord.

Cowboy, in that instant, caught the face of the Jeep driver, frozen in surprise that he wasn't dead.

Cowboy shook the clumsy weapon, and screamed at it. "*Open up, motherfucker!*"

26

Beeker. Beeker could help him! But the sounds of Cowboy's screams were hidden by the pounding of the battle around him. Cowboy looked up. Into the eyes of a gunner on the back of the third Indonesian Jeep. He was grinning, the bastard. He figured he was going to die but he'd decided he was going to take Cowboy with him. Cowboy wasn't so scary when he was holding a BAR that wouldn't fire. Cowboy was alone, in the middle of what a few days ago had been the thirteenth fairway of the Carib Hotel golf course. Cowboy looked into the eyes of the man who was going to kill him and thought, *This is what it is to die*. A cold wind was going to blow across that goddamn golf course and freeze his statistics off.

The man had him in his sights. Cowboy dove toward the Jeep, but he knew no hope. Calm amid the firing, the noise, the trembling of the earth beneath him he waited to feel the bullets' bite. The only thing that really bothered him was that he was going to die on a fucking golf course!

Cowboy felt the crosshairs of the gun on him. He hoped they were centered on his head. He wanted it quick. That would be a consolation. It would also be a consolation if he got it instead of Beeker. Or Tsali. They'd mourn him, he knew. Better he should die than either of them.

He closed his eyes, trying to wipe out the grin of victory on the gunner's face. He closed his eyes and began the worst waiting that he had ever known. Worse than that ditch by the side of the road. Much worse than anything Beeker could devise.

But nothing happened. Cowboy knew he should be dead by now. He should have been dead ten feet back. Cowboy had already waited too long for that gunner to squeeze.

He opened his eyes.

The gunner was grinning blood between his teeth and there was a big hole in the gunner's chest. He'd been hit from behind.

And there was something else too.

Silence.

Then, as if to fill that vacuum, Cowboy heard the noise of the surf half a kilometer away.

He looked cautiously around.

Bodies and blood and more bodies, and the lazily burning frame of a Jeep and a truck.

And there in the distance, but running—running toward him—Tsali Leaps Beeker, holding aloft the AK-47 with which he'd just saved Cowboy's life. And behind Tsali, smiling and holding an AK-47 herself, Delilah—cool and delicious.

Tsali never made it as far as Cowboy. Because Beeker had intercepted, and caught him up in his arms, and pressed him close to his chest, the BAR and the AK-47 dropping to either side.

27

The arrival of Beatrix VanderVolt back in New Neuzen was a state occasion. A band of high schoolers played the national anthem on an array of battered instruments. A smartly uniformed group of constables stood at attention as the stairway was wheeled up to the private 727 that Delilah had arranged. The prime minister stood in the door of the plane, waved regally in response to the cheering and the drumbeats, and then slowly descended the stairs. Behind her were two men, one tall and dark, the thick hair of his chest boiling up out of the open collar of his pressed khakis. The other short and blond, wearing the same outfit but managing somehow to look more like a nearsighted Boy Scout than a soldier.

The prime minister insisted on giving a dinner for the Black Berets and Delilah. Beeker accepted on the condition that there be no photographers, and no members of the press. At Delilah's quick connivance, it had been given out that Beatrix VanderVolt had engineered the defense of the island herself, using troops she'd chosen, hired, and trained under her personal direction. In exchange for this little puffery, the prime minister had agreed to allow the re-formation of New Neuzen's tiny military army. It hadn't taken much persuasion, and Delilah said to Beeker that the woman probably would have done it on her own.

All but three of the Indonesians were killed on the golf course. This trio managed to make it to the hotel, where they were captured by Rosie and Van Waring. The prisoners led them back to the cavern on the northwest side of the island. There, the six men who had served as female surrogates for the Black Palm were taken into protesting custody. Also, the money that the Black Palm had stolen in Europe was discovered. Beatrix VanderVolt would have nothing to do with it, but she saw to it that the two small chests were loaded onto Delilah's 727 without interference from her own customs people.

At the dinner, Harry sat on the prime minister's right, Marty on her left. And as usual, the meal degenerated into a long series of stories about how many people Marty had killed in the past week, and just how he'd done it. Rosie and Cowboy, who was still nervous about the fact that his BAR had jammed at the height of the battle, got royally plastered. Down at the far end of the table, Beeker, Delilah, and Tsali sat together, quietest of all. Beeker now and then couldn't help himself, but stared at the boy, and grinned and clapped him on the back. And Delilah smiled with a certain pleasure herself.

That night they had the Carib Beach Hotel pretty much to themselves. The tourists wouldn't be returning till the following day. Marty was down in the bar, telling his stories all over again to Harry, despite the fact that Harry not only had heard them before, he had taken part in them. Beeker guided drunken Rosie and Cowboy to bed, and then returned to his own room, in hope of having a quiet word alone with Tsali.

But Tsali wasn't there. Beeker looked through the suite once more, then went out on to the balcony. The hotel was dark, and the moon shone over the Caribbean. Something drew his attention to the left, and he saw, on the balcony of the room next to his, two quiet, silent figures. Tsali and Delilah. And to his astonishment, he saw that Delilah was signing to Tsali with her hands. As if she too were mute.

Or as if she didn't trust herself to speak aloud the words she wanted to say to him.

She was turned so that Beeker could see the motions of her hands. He was in the shadows. If she saw him, she made no sign that she did.

Do you know why Cowboy drank so much tonight? she asked the boy.

Tsali shook his head.

He thought he was dead, signed Delilah.

Tsali nodded his comprehension.

You saved his life, she went on. *Your father is very proud of you.*

Beeker deftly leaped over the railing that supported the two balconies. Tsali whirled around at the noise and movement. Delilah simply looked up—evidently she had known he was there all the while. She rose and went inside then, merely saying aloud, "I'll leave you two men alone . . ."

She closed the drapes. Father and son stood together on the balcony, with only the noise of the breakers on the white beach a hundred yards out.

"I am proud of you," said Beeker.

Tsali glanced away.

I lost a friend, the boy signed after a moment.

"Doc Wilhelm," said Beeker. "Cowboy told me about it. I'm sorry, Tsali. It comes with the territory, and there's nothing to say. Except that now the battles are over, it's time you grieved for him. For your teacher."

Tsali stood motionless, but suddenly tears gushed from his

eyes, and his chest was racked with choking sobs till it seemed that he wouldn't be able to breathe for his sorrow.

Beeker didn't turn away. He looked at his son, to show him that his grief, his tears, were a right and proper tribute to the dead man. And when Tsali's tears had subsided, Beeker did what Delilah had done. He reverted to the signs because his heart was too full for the words he had to speak.

Though you are truly my son, you have also become a man. I thank the God of the Cherokee that I was here to see it happen.